THE BOXCAR CHILDREN
SUMMER SPECIAL

THE MYSTERY AT THE BALLPARK

THE MYSTERY OF THE HIDDEN BEACH

THE SUMMER CAMP MYSTERY

created by
GERTRUDE CHANDLER WARNER

ALBERT WHITMAN & Company
Morton Grove, Illinois

The Boxcar Children Summer Special
created by Gertrude Chandler Warner.

ISBN 10: 0-8075-0885-3
ISBN 13: 978-0-8075-0885-5

For more information about Albert Whitman & Company,
visit our web site at www.albertwhitman.com.

Contents

THE MYSTERY AT THE BALLPARK

created by
GERTRUDE CHANDLER WARNER

Illustrated by Charles Tang

ALBERT WHITMAN & Company
Morton Grove, Illinois

The Mystery at the Ballpark
created by Gertrude Chandler Warner;
illustrated by Charles Tang.

ISBN 10: 0-8075-5341-7
ISBN 13: 978-0-8075-5341-1

For more information about Albert Whitman & Company,
visit our web site at www.albertwhitman.com.

Contents

CHAPTER 1

Tryouts

"But I'm not very good at baseball," Violet said to Henry. It was early evening and the Aldens were sitting on their front porch in Greenfield.

Henry, who was fourteen, gave his sister an encouraging smile. "Don't worry, Violet. All you need is a little practice." Ten-year-old Violet was a shy girl with long brown hair and a sweet personality.

"I'm excited!" Jessie said. "I was hoping someone would start a team in Greenfield."

"Who told you about it?" Violet asked.

"Michael and Nicole Parker," Henry said. "They just moved in down the street. They said the real estate agent told them about the team!"

"We have new kids to play with?" Benny asked excitedly. He tucked his legs under the porch swing and set it rocking. "How old are they?" Benny, age six, loved to make new friends.

"Michael's twelve and Nicole is ten," Jessie said. "They want us to go to the dugout with them tomorrow morning."

"What's a dugout?" Benny asked.

"That's the little shelter where the players sit while they wait for their turn to bat," Jessie explained.

"Are Michael and Nicole really good at baseball?" Violet asked. She still felt a little uncertain about playing.

"I don't think so," Jessie said, hoping to reassure her sister. "I think they just want to make friends with all the kids in the neighborhood."

"I think we should do it," Henry said. "It will be fun!"

"I want to be a pitcher," Benny chimed in. He jumped off the swing and threw an imaginary ball.

"It's too bad Soo Lee is away," Jessie pointed out. "She likes sports." Soo Lee was their cousin, and she had gone fishing with her father.

"I think it's time for us to make a trip into town to get you some equipment," their grandfather said, rising from his chair. Watch, the family dog, scampered happily toward the driveway. He loved riding in the car with the children.

"Yippee!" Benny grabbed Grandfather's hand. "Can I buy a baseball cap, too?"

"Of course," Grandfather said.

"We should make a list of what we need," Jessie said thoughtfully. Jessie was twelve and always liked to plan ahead.

"I can use my Hank Aaron glove," Jessie said excitedly. Aunt Jane had given Jessie the old autographed glove for her birthday, and Jessie treasured it. Although it was a little too large, she used it whenever she had the chance.

"I think a ball and bat will be enough," Henry said. "Mr. Warren said that the kids share equipment."

"Who's Mr. Warren?" Benny asked. He jumped in the front seat the moment Grandfather opened the car door.

"That's the coach. Michael met him earlier today," Henry explained.

"We have a real coach!" Benny was thrilled. He was going to be part of a team!

The next morning was bright and clear as the Aldens gathered around the kitchen table. "I want everyone to have a good breakfast," Mrs. McGregor said, passing Benny a plate of pancakes. Mrs. McGregor was the Aldens' housekeeper and had been taking care of the family for years.

"These look good!" Benny loved to eat. He filled his plate with pancakes and scrambled eggs.

Jessie noticed four new water bottles sitting on the kitchen counter. "Thanks for filling those with ice water," she said to Mrs.

McGregor. "I was going to do that after breakfast."

"You can help me finish the lunches if you'd like," Mrs. McGregor said.

"What are we having?" Benny asked, eyeing the clock. He decided he had time for one more glass of orange juice.

"All your favorites." Mrs. McGregor checked the brown paper bags. "Peanut butter and jelly sandwiches, apples, and brownies."

Benny grinned and pushed back his chair. "I can hardly wait till lunch!"

Ten minutes later, the Parker children knocked on the front door. Michael was tall with a friendly smile. His sister, Nicole, stood beside him, her long hair pulled back in a ponytail.

"Ready to go?" Michael asked.

"Yes we are," said Jessie eagerly. She and Henry had been throwing a ball around as they waited.

"Ready as I'll ever be," Violet said uncertainly. She was still a bit nervous.

"I know how you feel," said Nicole. "I'm not much of a ballplayer either."

When they reached the field, they found a large group of children milling around. Violet noticed that all the girls and boys seemed to be at least ten years old. She glanced down at Benny. Was he too young to play? He was very proud of the bat and ball Grandfather had bought him, and she didn't want him to be disappointed.

Just then, a tall, sandy-haired young man approached them. "Hi there. I'm Chuck Roberts, the assistant coach." He was carrying a clipboard and had a pencil tucked behind his ear. "I need your name, age, and what position you want to play. Let's start with you." He pointed to Nicole.

"Ohmigosh." Nicole looked flustered. "I'm Nicole Parker, I'm ten years old, and . . ." she glanced at her brother. "What position do I want to play?"

"You haven't played much baseball, right?" Chuck was looking at her thoughtfully.

"Neither have I," Benny piped up. He

tossed his ball in the air and caught it. "It looks like fun, though."

"It is." Chuck handed the clipboard to Nicole. "Just write down your names and ages, and I'll tell Coach Warren we've got some beginners."

"How do we know what position to play?" Nicole asked curiously.

"It all depends on what you're good at," Chuck said.

"What do you mean?" Benny looked up, squinting his eyes in the bright sunlight.

"Well, if you have a strong arm, you might want to be a third baseman, but if you've got quick feet and quick hands, you might want to play second base." Chuck waited while Benny carefully printed his name. "Does anyone know what a shortstop is?"

"The shortest person on the team?" Benny offered.

Everyone laughed. "The shortstop stands between second and third base," Jessie called out.

"That's right," said Chuck.

"I have a lot to learn," Nicole said. She

traced a circle in the dust with the head of her bat.

"Don't worry, that's what we're here for." Chuck started to move away, but Benny tugged on his arm.

"What do we do next?" he asked.

"After you've signed up, get in line for tryouts," Chuck told him.

"Tryouts?" Nicole and Violet exchanged a look.

Nicole was worried. "If this is a test," she muttered, "I sure hope I pass."

The Aldens, along with Michael and Nicole, lined up as Coach Warren led the tryouts. He watched carefully as the children took turns pitching.

"Remember," Chuck called to a shy-looking girl, "you need to throw hard, and you need to throw with confidence." He waited until she pitched three balls in a row and then pointed to Violet. "You're next."

Violet gulped. The new ball felt slippery in her hands, and she dropped it as she moved into position.

"Just a second," Chuck said, walking toward her. "Do you have a good grip on the ball?"

Violet looked up nervously, clutching the baseball tightly.

"Hey, relax," Chuck said. "Look, this is how you throw the ball." He demonstrated for her.

"Oh no!" Violet cried as her ball went only a few feet and then dropped to the ground.

"That's okay." Chuck looked sympathetic. "You'll get the hang of it in a few days. You just need some practice." He walked back toward Coach Warren.

Next it was Jessie's turn. She pitched three balls, and even though they didn't go as far as she wanted them to, Chuck seemed satisfied.

"I wish I could pitch like that," someone said behind her a moment later.

Jessie recognized the shy-looking girl who had been pitching before. "Thanks. I play a lot — I love baseball." She stuck out her hand. "I'm Jessie."

"My name's Ann." She had pale skin, with tiny freckles sprinkled across her nose. "I just hope I do better at hitting than I did at pitching."

"That's a nice bat you have."

"Thanks. It belonged to my father. See all these little notches?" She ran her hand along the polished surface. "Each one means he got a home run."

"Wow." Jessie peered at the bat. "He was a good hitter!" She glanced over at Violet who was standing at home plate, wielding her new baseball bat. "That's my sister," she said, nodding toward the field. They watched as Violet swung and missed three balls in a row. Jessie sighed. "I don't think she's got the hang of this yet."

"She'll be fine," Ann said. Both girls cheered when Violet hit the fourth ball with a loud whack. "See what I mean?" Ann asked with a grin.

"Lunch break, everyone!" Chuck Roberts yelled.

Jessie and Ann began walking around the edge of the field toward some picnic tables in the shade.

"I'll introduce you to the rest of my family," Jessie offered. "And to two new friends of ours."

"I'd like that," Ann said quietly. "I don't know anyone here."

"You will," Jessie assured her. "Just remember, we're a team!"

CHAPTER 2

A Special Job for Benny

"Do you think we'll make the team?" Jessie passed Benny a water bottle and watched as he tore into his peanut butter and jelly sandwich. All of the kids were sitting at picnic tables having lunch.

"I'm already on the team. I'm a batboy," Benny said proudly. He wasn't exactly sure what that meant, but he knew it was an important job.

"Benny's going to be helping Mr. Jackson, who's in charge of the equipment," Henry explained. Benny was too young to play on the team, so Coach Warren had decided to give him a special job to do.

"That will be lots of fun, Benny." Violet was happy that her younger brother was going to be included, but she wondered if he would like working with Mr. Jackson. She had met him a few minutes earlier and he seemed like a very cranky old man.

"But what about the rest of us?" Jessie persisted. "Do you think we have a chance?"

"I don't think I do," Ann said sadly. "I didn't pitch very well, and I missed two balls when it was my turn to bat."

"Don't be discouraged, Ann. Trying is what counts." Henry reached for one of Mrs. McGregor's brownies. "Chuck told me that Coach Warren looks for kids who are good team players. That's even more important than talent."

"What about you, Henry?" Michael spoke up. "I didn't see you doing any pitching or hitting today."

"I'm not going to be on the team," Henry began.

"What!" Violet was crushed. How could

her big brother not make the team! He was much stronger than anyone else on the field.

Henry chuckled. "Relax, Violet. I'm not going to be on the team, but I'm going to be part of it." He paused and looked around the table. "They decided that since I'm older than the other kids, I could help out. So I'm going to be Chuck's assistant."

"Wow!" Benny's eyes were wide with excitement. He was very proud of his brother.

"Then you can tell us what's going on," Nicole said. She twisted a lock of dark curly hair in her fingers. "Are they going to make the announcements after lunch, or will there be more tryouts?"

"No, tryouts are over. Chuck said that he and Coach Warren are going to go over the notes during lunch and come to a final decision."

"I feel nervous," Ann said quietly.

"Me, too," Nicole agreed. She looked at her brother, Michael, and knew that he was thinking the same thing. Now that they had made some new friends, they didn't want to lose them!

"Ready for some work?" Chuck appeared and patted Benny on the back. "I could use some help with the equipment."

"Sure thing!" Benny wolfed down the last bite of brownie and scrambled to his feet.

"Have you — I mean, has Coach Warren made up his mind yet?" Violet was so nervous her heart was thumping.

"He's still working on it," Chuck said casually. "We're going to post the list in half an hour or so, so you can relax for now."

"Relax!" Nicole blurted out. "You've got to be kidding!"

"Let's go, Benny. I'm going to give you your very first job to do."

"I'm ready!" Benny swung his legs off the bench and leaped to his feet. This was going to be fun!

They walked to the dugout, a small building that was open on one side to the field. Benches lined the open side, where the players sat during the game. Inside the dugout were several metal lockers and a cabinet to hold the equipment. Mr. Jackson sat on a bench inside, cleaning a glove with an oily rag. He was tall and thin, with wavy gray hair. He wasn't very friendly. When Chuck introduced Benny, he grumbled hello and then went back to what he was doing.

"Do you know much about baseball equipment?" Chuck asked.

"I know you need a ball and bat," Benny said.

"There's something else you need," Chuck said seriously, "and that's a batting helmet. Coach Warren wants everyone on the team to have one by tomorrow, and we're going to keep them in here." He pointed to a wooden cabinet. "For your first job, why don't you dust the shelves." He handed Benny a soft white cloth.

"Why do we need helmets?" Benny said, working quickly. He was glad that Chuck had chosen him to help out and wanted to do well.

"To protect your head when you're at bat or running the bases," Chuck explained. "You don't want to get hit by a ball." He coughed as a cloud of dust drifted up in his face.

"Sorry," Benny said. "These shelves are really dirty."

"That's okay. They haven't been touched since last season."

"There's an old bat in here," Benny said. He lifted it out and examined the knob. "Look, it must be a lucky bat. It has a number seven on it."

Chuck laughed. "It might be someone's lucky bat, but that's not what the number seven means. It means that the bat is twenty-seven inches long. That's about the right size for most kids."

Benny looked surprised. "I didn't know they came in sizes."

"They sure do. Never buy a bat that's too long. They weigh more, and they're hard to swing quickly."

"I'll remember that," Benny said eagerly. He loved working with Chuck. He was going to learn a lot!

"And buy a wooden bat. Aluminum bats cost a lot and you'll be changing bats as you get bigger."

"Right!"

"And never, never try to bat without your helmet. Coach Warren will really drum that into you."

"Got it!"

On the field, a blonde-haired girl walked over to the other Aldens as they were finishing their lunch. "Hi, I'm Susan Miller," she said with a friendly smile.

Henry scooted over for her to sit down, and everyone introduced themselves. "I saw you pitching before," he said. "You were very good."

"Thanks. I played a lot of baseball at camp last summer." She looked at Violet and Nicole. "What positions do you play?"

Violet looked embarrassed and Nicole giggled. "We're just beginners," Nicole explained. "We're laughing because people have been asking us that all morning."

"Sorry," Susan said. "I guess Coach Warren will figure out where to put everyone."

"Susan! Susan! I've been looking all over for you!" A tall woman rushed over to the table. Behind her was a woman who looked just like her except for her dark curly hair.

"Hi, Mom. Hi, Aunt Edna. I was just getting to know some of the kids." She introduced her mother and aunt to everyone at the table. Jessie noticed that Susan seemed a little downcast when her mother appeared, and suddenly got very quiet. Her mother, however, never stopped talking and asked everyone their names, ages, and how much playing experience they had.

"Are you one of Coach Warren's assistants?" Nicole asked.

Mrs. Miller's jaw dropped. "Why no, why would you ask that?" She flushed a little and Violet knew that she didn't like the question.

Nicole calmly answered, "You seem so interested in everything. I thought maybe you were helping to choose the team."

"Well, I . . . of course not!" Mrs. Miller said abruptly. "I'm just a parent." She put her arm around Susan. "My daughter is an excellent player, and I'm here to watch the tryouts." She looked impatiently toward a folding table where Coach Warren and Chuck were poring over scribbled pages of notes. "I wish they'd hurry up and make up their minds."

"Mom, this takes time," Susan said quietly. "They want to make sure they pick the right people for the right positions."

"How long can it take?" Mrs. Miller snapped. "I can think of several positions that you could play."

Susan managed to change the topic and Jessie was relieved. It was obvious that Mrs. Miller liked having things her way!

"Do you want to walk around the field with me?" Ann stood up. "I'd like to walk some laps while we wait for the news. It makes me edgy just sitting doing nothing."

"Sure, I'll come with you," Nicole said, gathering up her napkin and paper cup.

"Me, too," Violet said, jumping to her feet. Being around Mrs. Miller was making her very nervous.

"How do you like Greenfield so far?" Violet asked Nicole a few minutes later. The three girls were walking briskly around the outer edge of the field. Each one knew that if she were chosen for the team, she'd soon be running two or three miles along the same path every day.

"I like it a lot since we met all of you," Nicole said. "I thought it would take a long time to make new friends, but Michael said joining this team was a good way to get started."

"I'm glad he thought of it," Violet said. "But we'll still be friends, whether we make the team or not."

"Oh, I hope we do," Ann said suddenly. She stopped and peeled off her jacket. "I'm going to put this with my bat, and I'll catch up with you later, okay?" When she left, Nicole told Violet about her family, and Violet told her all about Grandfather and how he had found the Aldens living in a boxcar.

Nicole looked surprised. "You mean you were orphans, living on your own?"

Violet nodded. "We thought we wouldn't like our grandfather, but then he found us and took us into his house, and everything changed. He's the best grandfather in the whole world," she said. "We have a wonderful home, and a dog named Watch, and a really nice housekeeper, Mrs. McGregor, to take care of us."

"They're announcing the team!" a boy said, whizzing by them.

"Oh, let's hurry." The three girls jogged to the center of the field where Chuck was standing with his clipboard. Coach Warren was at his side, and he leaned over and whispered something in Chuck's ear. Chuck nodded, and then motioned for everyone to gather around him.

"First, I want to thank everyone for coming. I know you all tried your hardest."

Jessie glanced over at her sister, and noticed that she had her fingers crossed and had squeezed her eyes tightly shut. Jessie hoped that they would all be playing baseball together the following day.

"We have the final team list," Chuck said. "Anybody who isn't chosen for the team can still be a substitute player. They'll fill in if anyone gets sick or drops out." He shaded his eyes from the sun. "Okay, here goes: Alden . . ."

"Which one?" Violet blurted out, opening her eyes.

Chuck glanced at his list. "Both," he said. "Jessie and Violet."

"Yippee!" Jessie threw her arms around her sister. "We made it!" Both girls were still hugging each other when they heard Nicole's name called out. "Great! We'll all be together!" Jessie said, pulling Nicole into the circle.

"Michael Parker . . . Susan Miller . . . Ann Richmond . . ."

Violet was glad that the shy girl had made the team.

"Where *is* Ann?" Jessie asked.

"Look, there she is." Nicole pointed to Ann, who was running across the field toward them. Nicole started waving, and then stopped and frowned. "Something's wrong. She's crying!"

"Ann, what is it?" Jessie asked when Ann

reached them. Ann's eyes were red, and her face was streaked with tears.

"My dad's bat . . ." she sobbed. "It's gone! I think someone *stole* it!"

"Oh Ann, I'm so sorry," Nicole said. "We'll help you get it back."

Jessie and Violet exchanged a look. The Aldens had another mystery to solve!

CHAPTER 3

The Search

"Tell me exactly where you left it, Ann," Jessie said calmly. "We'll all work together and look until we find it." Jessie knew how important the bat was to Ann.

"I left it in the dugout," Ann said tearfully. "Chuck said it was okay to put our things in that big wooden cabinet."

"We'll spread out," Jessie said, scanning the field. The field was crowded with parents and kids making their way back to their cars. "Violet, why don't you get Benny and Henry to help you search the picnic area?" She turned to Nicole and Michael. "Could you two check the dugout again? Ann and I will cover the field."

Jessie and Ann walked quickly toward the center of the field, weaving in and out of the crowd. Twenty minutes later, Ann was ready to give up. "It's no use. We've gone over every inch of ground," Ann said, sniffling.

Henry and Benny caught up with them. Jessie knew from the look on their faces that they hadn't had any luck either.

Henry spoke first. "I'm sorry, Ann. We looked everywhere." He shrugged helplessly. "It seems to have vanished into thin air."

"We even asked Coach Warren and Chuck," Benny piped up. "And Mr. Jackson."

"No one even saw it?" Ann cried. "What am I going to tell my father?"

"It still might show up," Violet said, hugging Ann. "Someone might have taken it by mistake, and he or she will bring it back tomorrow."

* * *

That night at dinner, the Aldens celebrated with Grandfather. "I'm very proud of all of you," he said, looking around the table. "Two baseball players, a batboy, and an assistant coach."

"Not quite an assistant coach," Henry said, smiling, "but thank you, Grandfather."

"Did you learn much about baseball today, Benny?" Grandfather asked.

"I know I need a lot more practice," Benny said, reaching for a breadstick. "Chuck pitched some balls to me and I swung at them, but I didn't hit any."

"You know, I played a little baseball in my day," Grandfather said. "Maybe I can give you a few pointers before it gets dark."

"Yippee! Let's go!" Benny was ready to scramble off his chair, but Mrs. McGregor stopped him.

"Not so fast, young man. You wouldn't want to miss my hot apple pie with ice cream, would you?"

Grandfather laughed at the look on Benny's face. "Don't worry, Benny, we have time to do both. Enjoy your pie."

Later, at bedtime, Benny told Henry about all the tips Grandfather had given him. He had learned so many things! "Do you know what it means if you swing high one time and low the next time?"

"That you should play another position?" Henry teased him.

Benny made a face. "That you're probably closing your eyes. Grandfather was right. That's exactly what I was doing!"

"It's getting late, Benny," Henry said mildly. He knew his younger brother was very wound up. Benny really loved to talk!

"And do you know what else? It's okay to be afraid of getting hit by the ball."

"Is that so?" Henry asked.

Benny nodded. "Even major league players are afraid of getting hit." He yawned, and scooted down under the covers. "But you have to watch the pitcher, and when the pitcher throws the ball, watch the ball." He pulled the quilt up under his chin. "You have to watch the ball all the way. . . . to the bat." Benny's voice trailed off.

"I'll remember that," Henry said softly. Benny was sound asleep. Tomorrow was going to be a big day for all of them.

The next morning, Coach Warren divided the team into groups. Jessie, Ann, and Nicole found themselves working on fielding drills.

"Okay, everyone!" Chuck blew a sharp blast on his whistle. "You already know how to catch . . ."

"We do?" Ann muttered under her breath. She was upset because she still hadn't found her missing bat.

"So what I'm going to teach you is fielding, or getting ready to catch," Chuck continued.

"I just hope this is easier than pitching," Jessie whispered to Ann.

"One thing you can be sure of," Chuck went on, "baseballs are almost never hit right at the fielder." He casually tossed a ball in the air and caught it. "So that means you have to be ready to move. The best way to get ready is to face the batter. Stand with your feet apart, as far apart as the width of your shoulders."

Jessie took a step out to the side and hunkered down a little.

"That's good, Jessie," Chuck said. "Lean forward a bit. And Nicole, keep your weight on the balls of your feet."

"I don't know if I'll ever get the hang of this," Nicole said an hour and a half later. They were sprawled under an oak tree taking a break before learning some new drills.

"I never thought water could taste this good," Ann said, taking a long, cool drink. Susan Miller walked by, swinging her bat, and Ann suddenly sat bolt upright. "That's my bat!" she said under her breath.

"What?" Jessie looked up in surprise.

"My bat! Susan has my father's bat."

Ann started to scramble to her feet, but Nicole held her back. "Wait a minute. How can you be sure?"

"I'd recognize it anywhere," Ann said, her eyes flashing.

"But why would Susan take it?" Jessie said. "Her mother bought her all new equipment. Anyway, I can't believe she'd take something that didn't belong to her."

"I can't let her get away with it," Ann said, flinging Nicole's hand off her arm.

"Wait a minute. Let's make sure before you confront her." Jessie glanced over her shoulder. They waited until Susan set the bat against a tree and headed for the pay phone. "Now's our chance," Jessie said, as the three girls dashed across the field.

"She put tape on it," Ann said a minute later. She was clutching the bat, picking at a strip of thick black tape. "But this is it all right. Here are the notches underneath."

"Was she trying to disguise it?" Nicole asked.

"Maybe not," Jessie said. "Sometimes people put tape on the bat where they grip it."

"What do we do now?" Ann said quietly. "Susan's on her way back."

"We have to give her a chance to explain," Jessie said.

"This better be good," Ann said. She was clutching the bat tightly to her chest.

"Hi, everybody," Susan said.

Ann got right to the point. "This is my

bat," she said flatly. "I'd like to know how you got it."

Susan looked blank for a moment. "Your bat . . ." she stammered. "I didn't know. Honest."

"See these notches? My father put them on."

"But they were covered up with tape. I had no idea it was yours." She looked at Jessie for support. "Why would I take someone's bat?"

"Where did you get the bat?" Jessie said.

"In my locker. I thought the coach put it there for me." Her eyes were welling up with tears. "My mother bought me a brand-new bat but I left it at home today. I'd never take something that wasn't mine." She wiped her arm across her eyes and hurried across the field.

"Well, now what?" Nicole asked. "Are you going to tell Coach Warren?"

"I'm just glad I got my bat back," Ann said. "I'm not going to say anything."

Chuck blew the whistle just then, and everyone returned to practice. Chuck was helping Jessie practice catching fly balls, when he spotted her autographed glove. "It says Hank Aaron. Is this for real?" He examined the signature. "I guess it is." He slipped his hand inside the glove. "I've always been a fan of his."

When they broke for lunch, Jessie put her glove in her locker. Mr. Jackson had assigned each player a green metal locker. Henry and Violet joined her at the picnic table, and Benny came racing up with Michael and Nicole. Everyone was starving.

In between bites of her cheese and tomato sandwich, Nicole told everyone about Susan and the bat.

"At least she got her bat back," Violet said.

"But it doesn't solve the mystery of who took it," Henry said. "Not if Susan's telling the truth."

"I'm sure she is," Nicole said. "She was really upset. She was crying!"

"Well, let's all be extra careful." Henry advised. "Jessie, where's your glove?" he said suddenly.

"It's safe," she told him. "Put away in my locker."

Except Jessie was in for a surprise. When she returned to her locker after lunch, she saw the door swinging open.

"Ohmigosh!" Nicole blurted out. "Someone's been in your locker. Is everything okay?"

Jessie looked inside. The locker was empty. "No, it's not okay," she said, close to tears. "My glove's gone."

Violet came up behind her just then, and realized what had happened. "Oh, Jessie, I'm so sorry," she said. "What do we do now?"

Henry, who was right behind Violet, spoke first. His voice was low, his expression tight. "We catch a thief," he said grimly.

CHAPTER 4

A Fake!

"I'm sure your glove will turn up, Jessie," Violet said the next day. "After all, Ann found her bat, didn't she?"

In the hands of another player, Jessie thought. It was nine o'clock in the morning, and everyone was lined up to practice hitting.

"Be more aggressive, Susan," Chuck shouted. The blonde girl nodded and hit the ball again as Jessie watched. After a few more hits, Chuck signaled for the next player to step forward, and Susan dropped back to the end of the line.

"I think we're getting better," she said to Jessie. "At first I couldn't hit the ball at all. Now I'm getting two out of three."

"All our practice is paying off," Jessie said.

"Baseball is taking up a lot of my time," Susan said. She flexed the fingers on her right hand. They were cramped from gripping the bat too tightly. "I've had to let my painting and drawing slide."

"You're an artist?"

Susan looked a little shy. "My aunt's the real artist in the family. She gives me art lessons every week, but I've had to cut back since I started coming here."

The line moved forward then, and Violet tried gripping the bat the way Chuck had showed her: fingers half an inch away from the knob, with the middle knuckles lined up.

Meanwhile, Benny was getting some advice on baseball from Mr. Jackson. "Do you know how to tell if you've got the right bat, Benny?" The two were sorting through the equipment during the morning's practice.

Benny shook his head. "No, they all look alike to me." He put down a stack of helmets, hoping Mr. Jackson would go on talking. There was so much he could learn about baseball, and he didn't want to miss a word.

"I'll show you a little trick, son," Mr. Jackson said, handing Benny a shiny new bat. He positioned Benny's arm so Benny was holding the bat straight out in front of him. "Count to ten, Benny."

"One . . . two . . . three . . ." Benny had no idea what Mr. Jackson was up to.

"Getting a bit tired?" The bat sagged a little as Benny kept on counting. "That means it's too heavy for you. The secret is to hold the bat straight out for ten seconds. If your arm doesn't droop, it means it's the right weight." He handed Benny another bat. "Try this one."

"Wow! I bet you know everything in the world about baseball."

"I've been around the game a long time," Mr. Jackson said. "Seen a lot of changes in my day." He paused and rubbed his neck thoughtfully. "Of course, not all the changes are for the good."

"Like what?" Benny scooted up onto a

workbench, with his feet dangling off the edge.

"In my day, baseball was a boy's game," Mr. Jackson said gruffly. "Nowadays the girls all play." He swept a screwdriver and a saltshaker off the workbench into a drawer.

Benny started to reply, but Henry walked into the dugout just then with a pile of clean towels. What was wrong with girls playing baseball? he wondered. His sisters played!

Later that morning, Nicole and Violet decided to dash to a nearby store for lemonade. Although the day was sunny and warm, the field had been muddy and practice had been hard. "We have ten minutes for break," Nicole said a little breathlessly. "That's three minutes each way, and four minutes to buy the drinks." Coach Warren was very strict about breaks, and anyone who came back late had to run laps.

"Is it lunchtime?" a dark-haired woman asked when they entered the store. Violet recognized her from tryouts. She had been with Susan Miller.

"Not yet," Violet said politely. "We just

have a short break. Are you Mrs. Miller?"

"No, I'm Susan's aunt, Edna Sealy," Mrs. Sealy said.

"It seems like I've been waiting for hours." She looked disgusted. "How long can that stupid game go on?"

Nicole and Violet exchanged a look. Mrs. Sealy didn't seem to like baseball. So why did she bother coming to practice?

"Did you see Susan hitting this morning?" Violet asked. "She's doing much better. Chuck says she has a lot of talent."

"I guess you could call it that," Mrs. Sealy said sourly. "If you think it takes any talent to hit a ball with a stick. And no, I didn't see her play. I dropped her off this morning and have been doing errands ever since." She watched as the girls scooped up their drinks. "Tell Susan to try to finish early." She sighed. "I'd like her to get some painting in today." She walked to the window, and Violet noticed that her tennis shoes were caked with bright red mud. Where had she seen that strange color before? she wondered.

"We will," Nicole said, darting out the

door. Poor Susan, she thought. The coach had already told them that practice would be running late. Her aunt would really be upset.

The Aldens had lunch with their new friends, Nicole and Michael.

"I don't think I'll ever be a pitcher," Michael moaned. "My arm feels like it's ready to drop off." He rubbed his upper arm with the flat of his hand.

"I know what you mean," Violet said sympathetically. "I've got some sore spots, too. Chuck said that we'll get used to it."

She opened a bag of sandwiches and passed the first one to Benny, who looked like he was starving. "Oh, we forgot the apples."

"I'll go get them," Jessie said, scrambling to her feet. "They're in my locker."

She hurried back to the lockers, and smiled at Mr. Jackson, who frowned at her. "I forgot something," she explained, as she flung open the locker door. She reached in without looking and was startled when her hand touched something leathery. "What in the world — " she began. It was her glove!

Grabbing the glove and clutching it to her chest, she ran all the way back to the picnic table.

"You found your glove!" Violet cried.

"Someone returned it," Jessie said happily. She felt so relieved! It wasn't until she sat down and took a closer look at the glove that she gasped out loud. "Wait a minute," she said slowly, "this isn't my glove. It's a *fake*!"

"How do you know?" Henry said quickly. He reached for the glove and turned it over, examining the signature.

"Look at the handwriting," Jessie said in a quavery voice. She felt close to tears. "Someone tried to forge the signature." She shook her head angrily. "They didn't do a very good job."

"You're right," Henry said finally. "It does look different."

"And the color's wrong," Benny piped up.

"That's true," Jessie agreed. "My glove was a little lighter. It was faded from being in the sunlight."

"So somebody went to a lot of trouble to

make you think you got your glove back," Michael said. "But who?"

"And why?" Nicole added.

"Whoever stole it. I guess they wanted to cover up the theft," Jessie suggested.

"This makes two thefts in less than a week," Henry pointed out. "I think we're going to have to keep our eyes open."

"How did somebody sneak this into Jessie's locker?" Benny asked.

"I don't know," Henry said slowly. "Think hard, Benny. Was there anyone hanging around the dugout besides you and Mr. Jackson? It must have happened sometime this morning."

"That's right," Jessie agreed. "My locker was empty when I put the apples in at eight o'clock."

Benny scrunched his face in thought and finally shook his head. "Nobody. I didn't see anybody in the dugout." He paused. "Except for Chuck."

"Chuck wouldn't take the glove," Nicole said quickly. She liked the friendly young man who was giving them so much help.

"I don't think so either, but . . . he admired it," Jessie said. "He told me Hank Aaron was his favorite player."

Violet turned the glove over in her hand. It had a rough, grainy texture, and the leather was coarsened. She saw tiny white specks caught in one of the seams. "That's funny," she said. "This looks like salt."

"Salt?" Michael was interested. He reached for the glove and rubbed his fingers gently over the surface. "You're right. Someone rubbed salt into it, to break down the leather. You know, to make it look old."

"Salt!" Benny blurted out. He clapped his hand over his mouth.

Everyone stared at him. "What's wrong?"

Benny looked around nervously, and when he spoke his voice was hardly a whisper. "Mr. Jackson had a saltshaker on his workbench today. I saw him put it into the drawer just as Henry walked in."

Henry's face was serious. "Do you think he was trying to hide it?"

Benny shrugged. "I don't know. He didn't act that way."

"Well, of course he'd try to act casual," Nicole pointed out. "If he was really guilty, of course. He wouldn't want you to be suspicious."

"I wasn't," Benny admitted. "At least not then." He sat lost in thought. He just couldn't imagine that Mr. Jackson would steal Jessie's glove and then try to replace it with a fake one. Why would he do such a thing? Suddenly he remembered something. "Hey!" he said.

"What is it, Benny?" Henry asked.

"You know what?" Benny said, "Mr. Jackson doesn't think girls should play baseball!"

"What?" Jessie was outraged. "You're kidding!"

"No, it's the truth." Benny told them about his conversation with Mr. Jackson.

"How weird. Do you think *he* was kidding?" Violet asked. She had noticed that Mr. Jackson had never been too friendly to her, but she found it hard to believe he didn't want her on the team.

"I don't know," Benny said, his eyes solemn. "But does this have anything to do with stealing Jessie's glove?"

Henry took a deep breath. "Maybe. If he really wants the girls off the team, I suppose he could make things hard for them, one by one. First Ann, and her missing bat, and then Jessie, and the missing glove."

"Maybe he thinks if he causes enough problems for the girls, they'll all quit," Michael said.

Jessie was angry. "Then he doesn't know us. I'll play whether I get my glove back or not."

"We all will," Violet said encouragingly. "Anyway, Mr. Jackson might not even be the thief. It might be someone else."

"But who?" Benny asked.

Chuck blew his whistle for everyone to come back to the field. "I don't know. We'll have to think about it," Henry said.

Somehow they had to solve the mystery before anything else disappeared.

CHAPTER 5

The Bears

"Meet our new mascot," Benny said to Nicole and Michael the next morning. He proudly held up a battered teddy bear. Jessie had made the bear from old stockings back when they lived in the boxcar. "This is Stockings," Benny told them.

"Very nice," Nicole said, panting a little. She squinted a little against the bright sunlight. They were starting their morning practice by running laps around the playing field. "But why do we need a mascot?"

"To bring us luck," Benny said seriously.

"Baseball players always need something to give them good luck. Didn't you know that?"

"Sure," Michael said. He dropped back a little to keep pace with Benny. "Some players make sure they tie their shoelaces the same way before every game and eat the same thing for breakfast. They think it makes them play better."

Benny nodded. "That's why I brought Stockings. There won't be anything else missing around here. You'll see."

"Whatever you say, Benny," Michael said with a chuckle. "Are you going to carry him around all day?"

"I sure am!" Benny insisted. He hesitated. "Except for lunch. I'll have to put him down when I eat my sandwich."

After they finished their laps, Chuck and Benny laid a sheet of plastic on the ground so they could practice sliding into a base. The sheet of plastic was about four feet wide and twenty feet long. When it was wet, it became very slippery. It was just like zipping over a patch of ice.

Chuck explained that sliding was important because it helped you reach a base safely without getting tagged out by the baseman. And it was important to practice on the plastic so no one would get hurt. Everyone took their shoes off and Violet went first. She backed up a few feet and waited for Chuck to signal her to go. She felt a little nervous and wasn't sure she would do it right.

"Remember, Violet," he said, "it's just like falling."

"That's what I'm afraid of," she protested.

"But this is falling without getting hurt," Chuck pointed out. "Remember what I told you? If you do it right, you won't hurt yourself or the other players. Just relax and go with the fall."

"I'll try," Violet said.

"Go for it!" Susan Miller encouraged her.

"Keep your head up!" Henry yelled.

Violet took a deep breath and dashed toward the plastic strip. When her foot touched it, she immediately let herself go into a controlled fall, and tried to stay relaxed. It worked! Jessie applauded and Chuck gave her a thumbs-up sign.

All the players took turns on the plastic until Chuck was satisfied that everyone knew how to slide safely.

After lunch, Coach Warren called everyone together in the center of the field. "Listen up," he said. His face was ruddy from the sun and he tapped his clipboard. "I have a challenge for you. How'd you like to play a real game the day after tomorrow?"

"A real game?" Violet blurted out. To that point, they had just been practicing their skills. Chuck had gone over the rules of the game with them, but were they ready to take their positions on the baseball diamond?

"Do you mean it?" Benny asked excitedly. He was all set to root the team on to victory.

"Who would we be playing against?" Michael asked.

"Beginners, I hope," Nicole said under her breath.

"It's a team over in the next county, and they're starting out, just like you." Coach Warren looked down at his clipboard. "They call themselves the Pirates, and they've been playing for a month. Their coach called me last night, and asked if we'd be interested." He waited while everyone thought it over. "Well," he said finally, "are you ready for it?"

"We're ready!" Benny shouted. Everyone laughed. Leave it to Benny to speak for the whole team.

"Anybody else?" Coach Warren asked.

"I think we can do it," Henry volunteered.

"So do I," Michael spoke up.

"We might as well give it a try," Nicole said with a shrug.

"Let's do it," Susan Miller said.

"Count me in," Jessie offered, stepping forward.

"Me, too," Violet echoed. She was really getting better, and was excited at the thought of a real game.

Coach Warren grinned. "Great." He glanced at his watch. "Let's get to work, because game time is just two days away. Ten o'clock in Clarksville."

"So it's us against the Pirates," Henry said.

"Hey," Benny said suddenly, "what are we called?"

"That's a good point," Chuck said. "We need to choose a name."

"We better find one quick." Jessie looked at her teammates. "Anyone have any ideas?"

Benny thought hard. Tigers, ducks, wildcats, bulls . . . what would be a good name? Then he remembered his mascot, Stockings. "I've got it," he yelled. He held up Stockings. "We can be the Bears."

"The Bears. I like it!" Susan patted him on the back. Everyone started cheering, until Coach Warren blew his whistle. "Okay, now that we've got that settled, let's get back to practice." He tugged on the peak of his baseball cap and looked at them very seriously. "Play ball, Bears!"

Later that afternoon, a little four-year-old girl appeared at the edge of the field. She was wearing a pink sundress, and holding Mr. Jackson's hand.

"This is my granddaughter," Mr. Jackson said proudly, when Jessie and Benny wandered over during a break. "Her name's Sarah."

"Hi, Sarah." Jessie bent down so she was

on eye level with the little girl. "That's a pretty doll you have." She pointed to a Raggedy Ann doll that Sarah was clutching.

"She loves dolls," Mr. Jackson said. "Stuffed animals, too. Her room's full of them."

Sarah stayed for the rest of the practice, watching as Jessie and Violet worked on their pitching and fielding.

"I'll never get these ground balls," Violet said. She shook her head as the third ball in a row skirted past her ankles.

"Remember what Henry said," Michael reminded her. "Hold your glove with the fingers to the ground. That way you can scoop up the ball as it rolls into the glove."

"And don't shut your eyes," Jessie reminded her.

"I'll try," Violet promised. This time she didn't turn her head or squeeze her eyes shut. She looked straight at the ball, dropped to one knee and scooped it up as it whizzed right into her glove. "I got it!" she said happily.

Before practice broke up, Coach Warren gathered everyone together for a little pep talk. The sun was setting and a soft breeze swept over the playing field. The Aldens were sitting cross-legged on the grass as the Coach paced up and down in front of the players.

"You've been working hard," he said, "and I think we've got a good team." He glanced at Henry and Benny. "And I don't mean just the players. Our two special assistants have done a great job." Benny looked at Henry and broke into a wide grin.

"But I want to give you a little advice." He clapped his hands behind his back and strode up and down. "Do you know the first rule of baseball?"

Susan called out. "Keep your eye on the ball?"

Coach Warren nodded. "That's part of it. I was thinking of the bigger picture." He paused and looked at the circle of players. "Something I've had to remind you of from time to time."

Nicole guessed it. "Keep your mind on the game?" Just yesterday, Chuck had caught her daydreaming while she was waiting for the pitcher to throw the ball.

"That's it," the coach said approvingly. "I want you to think about the game *all* the time."

"I think we do. Usually," Michael spoke up. He grinned. "But I guess we all can try harder."

"That's the spirit," Coach Warren said. "Remember, there may be innings when you have nothing to do in the outfield. Even if your body has nothing to do, keep your mind working. Watch every pitch and be ready. The hitter may send the ball right to you. Yell to your teammates to encourage them. Talk to them about the game . . . how many outs . . . who is at bat . . . who's backing up the players on the infield."

Violet scuffed her toe in the soft red earth. She knew the coach was right. Sometimes when she was waiting to take her turn at bat, she drifted off into a world of her own.

"Don't listen to the crowds," Coach Warren went on. "Don't talk to anyone but your teammates. Don't be thinking of anything but the ball game. Can you do that?"

"You bet we can!" Benny leaped to his feet and everyone joined him. "Nobody can stop the Bears!"

Coach Warren looked at Chuck. "I think we've got ourselves a team."

Half an hour later, the Aldens, along with Michael and Nicole, stopped at the grocery for a quick drink before heading home. It was very warm out, and Violet was longing for a lemonade.

"How do you feel about playing the Pirates?" Violet asked. Nicole acted very confident on the outside, but she suspected that her new friend was feeling as nervous as she was.

"A little scared," Nicole admitted. "I probably wouldn't say that to anyone but you, though."

"Me, too," Violet paid for the drinks and carried them back to the small table where the rest of the group was waiting. A few minutes later, they noticed Chuck buying a package of gum in the front of the store. He was with a boy about eleven years old, and didn't see the Aldens.

"Who's that with Chuck?" Nicole whispered.

"I don't know," Henry said.

After Chuck and the young boy had left, Benny patted his duffel bag. "Stockings brought us good luck today," he said proudly. "Nothing else missing, and we get to play another team."

"Just make sure you bring him the day after tomorrow," Violet said. "I'm going to need all the good luck I can get."

"So where is our mascot?" Nicole asked.

"Right here." Benny reached into his duffel bag. "I'll bring him out so he can join us." He groped inside the bag, and his expression suddenly became alarmed. "Oh no!" he wailed.

"What's wrong?" Violet said quickly.

Benny took everything out of the duffel bag and turned it inside out on the seat. There was no sign of the stuffed bear. "He's gone," Benny said hoarsely. "Stockings is gone!"

"Oh, no, Benny! Are you sure?" asked Jessie.

Benny frowned. "Yes," he said. "Someone *took* him!"

Nicole shook her head in dismay. A stolen bat, a stolen glove, and now the team mascot was missing. What did this mean for the Bears?

CHAPTER 6

A Long Way to Clarksville

"I'm so nervous I don't think I can hold onto the bat," Violet whispered to Nicole.

Nicole nodded. "My hands are slippery, too. And I feel like I swallowed a whole jar full of butterflies." She tugged the visor down on her cap. "Let's just hope the other team is as scared as we are."

It was eight in the morning and everyone was gathered at the playing field. Violet tried to ignore the fact that her stomach was growling. She had barely touched the hot oatmeal that Mrs. McGregor had prepared that morning. She had been too excited thinking about the game! Would she remember everything Chuck had told her? Would she score a run? Would the team be proud of her?

Benny was the only one who seemed calm. He had polished off two bowls of oatmeal and a double helping of French toast.

Now Henry stood next to his little brother and ruffled Benny's hair. "How's it going, Benny?"

"Okay, I guess." Benny scuffed his toe in the soft red earth. "I miss Stockings, though. And today's our very first game. We need him for luck!" Benny had checked the dugout that morning, hoping to find the stuffed bear.

"Maybe Stockings can still bring us luck," Violet said. "From wherever he is." She knew her little brother was disappointed. "After all, he's still our mascot, even if he's not with us."

Benny brightened. "That's right," he said. "I never thought of that."

"Let's hit the road, everybody!" Chuck blew his whistle and slid open the doors on

Coach Warren's navy blue van. All their equipment was packed in a metal container on the roof.

Violet, Jessie, and Nicole piled into the back of the van and Benny slid in next to them. Benny loved to ride in a car and hoped everyone would sing or play games once they got under way.

When all the players were settled and had fastened their seatbelts, Coach Warren turned the ignition key. Nothing happened. He frowned and tried again. "That's funny," he said. After a third time, he turned to Chuck. "It's dead. Completely dead."

Chuck glanced at the gas gauge. It was full. "Why don't you give it another try?"

After a few more minutes, Coach Warren swiveled around in his seat. "I'm afraid we've got a problem, gang. This van isn't going anywhere." When everyone groaned, he held up his hand. "Don't worry, all we need to do is switch vans. Just give me a minute and I'll get the keys to the red one. It's a little smaller, but at least it'll get us there." When he disappeared into the office, Benny sighed.

"You don't think this happened because Stockings is missing, do you? Maybe we're in for a string of bad luck."

"Of course we're not," Violet reassured him. "Everything is going to be fine. We'll switch vans and we'll be on the road in a few minutes. You'll see."

Except it wasn't that simple. When Coach Warren reappeared a few minutes later, his face was red. "I can't understand it," he said, when Chuck hopped out of the blue van to meet him. "I can't find the keys."

"They're on the hook by the door," Benny said. He had noticed that the coach always kept them there.

"Not this time," Coach Warren said. He thought for a moment. "When's the last time you saw them there, Benny?"

Benny shrugged. "Maybe yesterday or the day before. But not today."

"That's what I was afraid of." Coach Warren scratched his head. "I don't understand what could have happened to them."

"Have you checked your pockets?" Henry asked.

The coach turned his pockets inside out but there was no sign of the missing keys. He turned to Chuck. "Did you happen to notice them this morning?"

"I haven't been in the office," Chuck said.

Wait a minute — that's not true, Jessie thought silently. She had noticed Chuck coming out of the office when she crossed the field. Had he forgotten? Or was he lying? She closed her eyes and tried to remember exactly what she had seen. Yes, she decided. The sun had been in her eyes, but she had seen Chuck walking out of the office with someone right behind him. Who was it? Suddenly the figure came into focus in her mind. It was Mr. Jackson. Both of them had been in the office. Could one of them have taken the keys? But why?

"We'll have to find those keys," the coach muttered. "And if they don't turn up, we'll have to get this van started."

When Chuck and Coach Warren went back into the office to search again for the keys, Henry opened the hood on the van.

"What are we looking for?" Nicole asked,

peering at the engine. "I wonder if the van needs oil . . ." Henry suddenly gasped. "Look at this!" he pointed to a jagged set of cables. Someone had sliced right through them!

"What is it?" Michael and Jessie hurried over.

"Someone's cut the cables to the battery," Henry explained. "No wonder the engine wouldn't start."

"But who would do something like that?" Violet was shocked. She couldn't believe that anyone would really want to hurt the team. The thefts were one thing, but now a whole game was at stake!

Henry showed Chuck and Coach Warren what he had discovered. "It's hard to believe," the coach said as he stood peering at the jagged ends of battery cable.

"I guess there's no way it could have happened accidentally?" Jessie said softly.

"I'm afraid not." Chuck shook his head.

"Looks like someone doesn't want us to get to Clarksville," Coach Warren remarked.

"Could it be someone on the Pirates team?" Michael asked.

"No chance of that." The coach took off his baseball cap and wiped his brow. "I talked to Coach Evert last night, and they can't wait to beat the pants off us." He smiled grimly. "They're already planning a victory pizza party for after the game."

Benny was angry. "How do they know they're going to win? We've got the best team around!"

"I think so, too, Benny," Coach Warren said. "But we can't prove it if we can't get to the game."

"How about your pickup truck, Chuck," the coach said suddenly.

"My truck?" Chuck looked doubtful. He glanced at the truck parked at the edge of the field. But then he brightened. "All right. We can't miss our first game."

Coach Warren slapped Chuck on the back. "Okay, team, let's a get a move on. We've got a game to play!"

Henry helped Chuck unload the equipment from the van and hand it to the players. "Two people can sit up front with me," Chuck announced, "and everyone else can pile in the back. There's a couple of blankets back there. Spread them on the bed of the truck so you don't get dirty."

Within minutes the truck was loaded, and Susan was wedged in between Jessie and Violet in the back of the truck. "Aren't you coming with us, Coach?" Jessie asked in surprise.

"I want to wait around for the road service. I called them when the van wouldn't start. Don't worry," he added. "Chuck will take good care of you, and I'll get to Clarksville in plenty of time."

Chuck made a thumbs-up gesture and pulled smoothly out onto the highway. "This is fun," Benny said, leaning against Violet. It was a warm day, and he loved to ride in the open air.

"Anybody hungry?" Susan asked. "Besides you, Benny," she added, and everyone laughed. She opened a large plastic bag of brownies and passed it around.

"These are great," Violet said, biting into

one. "Where did they come from?"

"My aunt made them," Susan replied. "She dropped them off before we started loading the van."

They had been driving for over half an hour, when Chuck suddenly pulled to the side of the road.

"What's wrong?" Nicole asked. Henry slid out of the front seat. "Chuck just wants to study the map," he explained.

"You mean we're lost?" Benny wailed. "I knew it. It's all because Stockings is missing."

"We're not lost, Benny," Chuck said. He spread open the map on the hood of the truck. "I just need to get my bearings."

"Where are we?" Nicole asked. They were on a dusty country road, bounded by farmland. In a nearby field, a group of black and white cows stared at them curiously.

"I don't know for sure," Chuck admitted.

"That means we're lost," Benny whispered.

"Do you know if we're even on the right road to Clarksville?" Violet asked. She was already nervous about the upcoming game, and it seemed like they were in the middle of one disaster after another!

"Not really," Chuck admitted.

"Maybe Coach Warren is already there," Michael said. "Maybe he's wondering where we are."

Chuck groaned. "I hope not." He held the map up and stared at a rusty road sign. "Route seven," he said, shaking his head. "That's not even on the map."

"Could we retrace our steps?" Henry suggested. "I think we left the main highway about ten minutes ago. Remember when we passed the fruit stand? We could go back there and get directions."

"Good idea," Chuck agreed. "I just hope we can find it."

They piled back into the truck, and Jessie glanced at her watch. They had been on the road for forty-five minutes and Chuck didn't even know where they were! And now they were heading for a fruit stand that might be impossible to find. How could so many things go wrong?

She looked at Benny, who had his eyes tightly closed. "What's wrong?" she whispered.

"I'm sending a secret message to Stockings wherever he is," Benny said softly. "We need a mascot right *now*."

Nicole overheard the conversation and smiled. "Tell Stockings we're counting on him," she said. She shifted her weight as the truck bounced along the bumpy road. "Because I've got the feeling that it's going to be a long, long way to Clarksville!"

CHAPTER 7

Play Ball!

"Just play your best," Coach Warren said an hour later as the team huddled around him. "That's all anybody expects of you." The van had been fixed and he'd made it to Clarksville before the others.

Chuck had gotten lost three more times, but the Bears had finally arrived, and the big game was about to begin. Everyone's nerves were on edge.

"And be a good sport, whether you win or lose," Chuck added. Jessie nodded, but she was beginning to wonder if the game was doomed from the start. So many things had gone wrong! She nervously checked out the opposing team. They all looked so confident! A girl close to her own age was taking practice swings with her bat, and the pitcher was throwing pitches to the catcher.

"They look pretty good, don't they?" Nicole said under her breath. She didn't want to admit it, but she was feeling a little nervous. Would doing her best be good enough?

Coach Warren had assigned their positions at the last practice. Jessie was at first base, Ann at second, and Michael at third. Susan was playing shortstop. A boy named Tom was pitching and his brother Steve was catching. Nicole and Violet were in the outfield with a boy named Bobby.

The Pirates were batting first, so the Bears ran to take their places on the field.

Once the game got under way, Violet felt some of her nervousness vanish. The Bears played well, and soon it was their turn to bat. When Violet came up to bat, she was thrilled to hear a satisfying *crack* as the bat hit the ball. Henry had told her that there

was no other sound in the world quite like it, and he was right!

Violet watched as the ball flew out toward center field, and she raced around the bases. Rounding first base she saw Coach Warren waving her on. She headed to second base and saw that the center fielder hadn't caught the ball, so she ran hard to third base. As she reached third she saw that the center fielder had thrown to second base, and the second baseman had dropped the ball. Violet took a deep breath and ran as hard as she could. As she tagged home plate she heard her teammates cheering. She'd hit a home run!

Jessie's big moment at first base came late in the game. The Pirate batter hit a hard grounder along the first base line. Jessie charged into action. She snatched up the ball and stepped on first base just before the runner.

"Way to go, Jessie!" Chuck yelled from the sidelines. She looked over and saw him give her the thumbs-up sign. I did it! she thought happily. Suddenly what Coach

Warren said earlier made sense. It didn't really matter if the Bears won or lost. All she had to do was do her best!

As the game went on, it was obvious that the Pirates had more experience than the Bears, and had practiced a lot. The Bears managed to keep up at first, but in the last inning the Pirates scored two runs to win the game.

The final score was Bears 5, Pirates 7. The two coaches shook hands, and the Bears headed toward the van.

"You mean that's it? It's over?" Benny said. He looked sad.

"Don't worry, Benny," Henry said. "We can always play them again." He took a long swig of water from Benny's bottle.

"I wanted us to win *now*," Benny said. He immediately thought of Stockings. He knew everything would have turned out differently if his mascot had been with them.

"You should feel good about yourselves," Coach Warren said as they piled into the van. "You did a great job, especially for your first real game."

"I made a ton of mistakes," Jessie said.

"Me too," said Nicole.

"That's okay. A good player learns from her mistakes. She practices harder to keep from making the same mistakes again. And that's what I expect you to do."

"I think he just said that to make us feel better," Nicole said to Chuck when Coach Warren moved away.

"No, he really means it," Chuck said seriously. "We all make mistakes, and hey, what would baseball be without errors and strikeouts?"

"Even big-name players strike out," Henry pointed out. "Nobody's perfect."

The next morning, the Aldens arrived at the dugout early, and Benny headed for the locker room. He was surprised to see Mr. Jackson fumbling with the combination lock on his locker.

"Oh, hello, Benny," Mr. Jackson said nervously, smoothing his gray hair. "I didn't hear you come in." He quickly moved away from the locker and wiped his hands on his overalls.

"What are you doing?" Benny asked curiously.

"Just checking the lockers," Mr. Jackson answered. He tried to smile, but his voice was tense.

"What for?" Benny persisted.

Mr. Jackson avoided looking at him. "Well, I . . . I'm thinking of repainting them," he stammered. "The paint's getting pretty chipped in spots, you know."

Benny looked at the gleaming row of bright green lockers and frowned. Chuck had told him that the lockers had been freshly painted a few months ago! Was Mr. Jackson lying to him? Was he really trying to break into his locker?

Later that morning, Jessie stopped to refill her water bottle and saw Mr. Jackson deep in conversation with Mrs. Sealy.

"I can't wait to see the look on Coach Warren's face," Mr. Jackson said.

"Neither can I," Mrs. Sealy agreed. "He's going to be in for the shock of his life."

Chuck blew his whistle just then, signaling the end of break time, and Jessie returned to the playing field. Were Mr. Jackson and Mrs. Sealy plotting something? Mrs. Sealy called it "the shock of his life." Were they going to do something that would embarrass Coach Warren? Surely neither one of them would have any reason to sabotage the team, would they? But what was the big secret? Jessie thought about it all morning, and couldn't come up with any answers.

It wasn't until they were eating lunch at the long picnic table that Nicole nudged her. "What's wrong?" she asked. "You're so quiet!"

Jessie hesitated. Was this the right time to bring up what was really bothering her? She glanced around the table. Only Nicole and Michael had joined the Aldens for lunch. The others had preferred to sit under the shade of a giant elm tree. Maybe if they all put their heads together, they could come up with an explanation.

"I think we need to clear the air," she said softly, and everyone turned to look at her. "There've been some strange things going on lately . . ." she began.

"I'll say," Benny interrupted her. "Some-one's been going around stealing teddy bears!" He missed Stockings and continued to look for him every day.

"I know, Benny," she said sympatheti-cally, "but I'm talking about more than just teddy bears."

"Weird things have been happening right from the start," Henry spoke up. "Remem-ber when Ann's bat was missing and ended up in Susan's locker?"

"And that was just the beginning," Violet said. "Jessie's glove was taken, and someone tried to trick her with a phony one."

"I never did get back my glove," Jessie said.

"I think it will turn up." Nicole gently squeezed her friend's arm.

"Yeah, maybe the same person who took your glove took Stockings," Benny piped up. "Maybe they'll feel so bad about taking them, that they'll return them both."

"And we nearly missed the game with the Pirates yesterday because so many things went wrong." Michael looked serious. "First someone cut the cables to the van, and then the keys were missing."

"Plus Chuck got lost a lot out in the country," Violet reminded him. "I'm surprised we made it there in time."

"Do you think it's just a string of coincidences?" Nicole asked. She took a bite of her sandwich. It seemed hard to believe that someone would really want to sabotage the team.

"I think it's more than that," Henry said. "So many things have happened that it seems like more than just a run of bad luck."

"Something else happened at the game," Michael said suddenly. "I didn't think of it before, but did anyone notice number thirty-eight on the Pirates team? A short kid with sandy hair?"

"I think I did," Benny said. "What about him?"

"I've seen him before." Michael paused and looked around the table. "All of us have. He was buying a soft drink with Chuck the other day in the store."

"That's right!" Violet burst out. "I knew he looked familiar!"

"But what does that mean?" Jessie asked. "Do you think Chuck is involved somehow in everything that's gone wrong?"

"I hate to think so," Henry told her.

Jessie nodded. "He said he hadn't been in the office when the keys were missing, but he was lying. I saw him walk out of the office a few minutes earlier, and Mr. Jackson was with him."

"Wow," Benny said softly. "Mr. Jackson might be involved, too."

"Why do you say that, Benny?" Henry asked.

Benny told them about Mr. Jackson snooping around his locker that morning.

"There's something else you don't know," Jessie said. "I heard a really strange conversation between Mr. Jackson and Mrs. Sealy this morning. It sounded like they were planning a surprise for Coach Warren — but not the kind of surprise you'd look forward to," she said grimly.

"Mrs. Sealy said she hates baseball, but she's always around," Nicole pointed out.

Violet frowned. "A lot of things about her don't make sense." Suddenly she remembered something else. "Remember when we saw her in the store that day and she said she hadn't been on the playing field? She wasn't telling us the truth! I *know* she'd been over here. She had red mud all over her shoes."

"You know, she must have been here when the van keys were missing, too," Nicole added.

"How do you know that?" Michael asked.

Nicole leaned forward eagerly. "Because Susan passed around a bag of brownies in the truck. She said her aunt had dropped them off for us that morning."

"That's right!" Jessie said. "So now we have three suspects, Chuck, Mrs. Sealy, and Mr. Jackson." She paused. "But I still can't figure out why any one of them would want to hurt the team."

"Mr. Jackson doesn't think girls should play baseball," Benny piped up.

"And Mrs. Sealy thinks Susan is wasting her time playing with us," Nicole offered. "She thinks she could be painting pictures."

"What about Chuck?" Benny asked.

Henry shrugged. "Maybe Chuck is secretly rooting for the other team because he has a friend — that little boy — who plays for them."

There was a long silence. "I think we have a long way to go before we solve this mystery," Jessie said.

"You're right," Violet told her. "But let's do it before anything else gets stolen."

CHAPTER 8

Henry Has an Idea

On Saturday morning, the Aldens trooped into the kitchen for an early breakfast. "I made waffles," Mrs. McGregor said as they settled around the oak table. "I know you want to get an early start for the fairgrounds." It was the day of the annual Greenfield flea market, and the children had invited Michael and Nicole to join them.

"What's a flea market, anyway?" Benny asked, pouring a tall glass of orange juice.

"It's like a giant yard sale," Jessie told him.

"People come from all over town and set up booths to sell things."

"What kind of things?"

"Just about everything. Furniture and dolls and antiques . . ."

"Oh." Benny looked disappointed.

"Cheer up, Benny," Violet said teasingly. "There will be lots of good things to eat, like homemade cookies and cakes and doughnuts."

"Oh, *good*!" Benny said, polishing off a waffle and reaching for another. "Then I know I'll like it."

Half an hour later, they met Michael and Nicole and headed for the fairgrounds. "This is going to be fun," Nicole said. "I can hardly wait to get there."

"And guess what," Michael spoke up. "Did you see the notice in today's paper? Someone's selling baseball cards and autographs!"

"Let's head there first," Henry said.

The fairgrounds were crowded when the children arrived. Everyone was excited by a display of gingerbread houses. "Oh, they're pretty," Nicole said. "They look just like something out of Hansel and Gretel."

"But I bet they're really expensive," Violet said. She had brought her allowance money with her in case she wanted to buy something.

"Maybe we can learn to make them ourselves," Jessie suggested. The Aldens always loved to figure out how to do things on their own.

Benny asked the woman behind the booth, "Can you eat the houses?"

She laughed. "I certainly hope not. Each one of them took almost a whole week to decorate."

"C'mon," Henry said, putting his arm around his younger brother's shoulders. "Let's take a look at those baseball cards."

A large group was gathered around the baseball card vendor's booth, and Michael recognized a familiar face. "See that woman in the red dress?" he whispered to the others. "Isn't that Susan's aunt — the one who's always hanging around the field?"

Nicole watched as a dark-haired woman

backed out of the crowd and headed toward another booth. "That's her, all right. I wonder what she was doing at this booth?"

"It can't be because she likes baseball," Jessie said. "She thinks it's a waste of time."

"Well, I think it's the most fun game in the whole world," Benny said loudly.

"You're right," Henry said, laughing. "Now let's see the cards for ourselves."

They had been sorting through bins of cards for a few minutes when Benny suddenly grabbed Jessie's arm. "That's it!" he said hoarsely.

"That's what?" Jessie said blankly. She was looking at a baseball card that pictured Hank Aaron and listed his 733 home runs.

"Your glove!" Benny said, continuing to tug at her. "The one Aunt Jane gave you."

"What — where?" Now he had her full attention.

Benny pointed silently to a slightly battered glove just out of reach on a display shelf. The autograph was clearly visible — Hank Aaron.

"Can I see that glove — the one on the

left?" Jessie asked the man running the booth. She was so excited her hands were trembling. How in the world had her glove ended up here? Had someone stolen it from the dugout and sold it?

"This is a nice glove. I can give you a good price on it."

Jessie turned it over thoughtfully in her hands. It certainly looked like her glove! But she wasn't sure what to say. She couldn't accuse the man of stealing it! "I . . . I had a glove just like this one," she said finally. "My aunt gave it to me."

"You mean you had a glove signed by Hank Aaron," the man said in a friendly voice.

"That's right!" Jessie said.

"So do lots of people," he replied, arranging a stack of baseball caps.

Jessie was puzzled. "What do you mean?"

"The big-name players sign lots of gloves. Everybody knows that."

"I didn't," Jessie said softly. She slipped her hand inside the glove. There was a little rough spot inside that rubbed against her

knuckle — just like her glove. Was it hers? And anyway what could she do? Even if it was, there was no way she could prove it.

"How much is it?" Henry asked. He had seen the look on his sister's face, and he was determined to buy the glove for her.

But when the man told them the price, it was very high.

"Oh, no," Violet said softly. "Mine was stolen." She knew there was no way they could afford that. "Maybe if we all saved for it," she began doubtfully.

"You say you had a glove that was stolen?" the man asked Jessie. When she nodded, he went on, "That's really a shame. Tell you what I can do. I'll set this one aside until you've earned the money."

"Really?" Jessie asked, her face lighting up. "Thank you."

Later that afternoon, the children visited a booth filled with beautiful leather belts and handbags. Violet ran her hand over a tan belt, so soft it felt almost buttery. A young girl with a ponytail sitting on a stool said proudly, "I made that one myself."

"It's so pretty," Violet said. "Look, Benny, it has a cowboy design carved into it."

Benny touched the belt. "It's nice. How did you get it so smooth?"

"I have a secret ingredient," the girl told him smilingly. She reached for a saltshaker on the countertop. "Salt."

"Salt?" Violet and Benny said together.

The girl nodded and stood up. "When you want to soften leather, you soak it for awhile and then rub salt into it. Instead of being hard and stiff, it makes the leather soft, as if you've been wearing the belt for awhile."

Benny stood silently for a moment, thinking. That was what Michael had said when they'd found traces of salt on Jessie's glove — the fake one that someone had put in her locker. And Mr. Jackson always kept a saltshaker in the dugout. Was he the guilty one?

Toward the end of the day, the children ate hot dogs in the shade.

"Do you think that was really your glove?" Nicole asked her.

Jessie shrugged. "I'm not sure. It certainly looked like it and felt like it."

"But that still doesn't explain how it got here," Violet pointed out.

"We're never going to figure that part out," Michael said. "At least not until we catch the thief." He sipped some apple juice through a straw.

"I've been thinking about that." Henry leaned forward. "Maybe we shouldn't just sit back and wait for the thief to strike again."

"But what can we do?" Violet asked. "We can't catch him until he commits another crime."

Henry snapped his fingers. "That's it, exactly. And you know what? We can set him up so he *has* to commit another crime. He just won't be able to resist."

Michael looked interested. "You mean we offer him something, and once he grabs it — "

"We grab him!" Nicole finished for him.

"A trap!" Henry said. "You've got it." He looked at the other children. "So what do you think?"

"What could we offer him?" Jessie asked. "It would have to be something he'd really like to have."

"He already has my teddy bear," Benny said sadly.

Jessie put her arm around him. "I have a feeling we'll get Stockings back for you, Benny, even though I can't promise." She paused. "I think we have to offer him something to do with baseball. After all, look what he's stolen — a bat, a glove, and a mascot."

"And there's more than that going on," Nicole pointed out. "He took the keys to the van, cut the battery cables, and almost made us miss our game with the Pirates."

"You keep saying 'he,' " Michael reminded her. "We don't know that for sure. It could be a she."

"That's true," Violet agreed. "But there's one thing we're sure of. Everything is somehow connected to baseball."

"And that's exactly the way we trap him or her," Henry said. "We offer the thief some kind of baseball trophy, or autograph. Something that he just can't pass up."

"I know," said Jessie. "Something we saw back there." She jerked her thumb toward the row of booths.

"What's that?" Benny asked.

Jessie smiled. "Something small, something easy to hide, something easy to steal. And something the thief would really like to have if he likes baseball."

Benny scrunched his forehead. What was Jessie getting at? "I got it!" he said suddenly. "A baseball card. We're going to catch him with a baseball card."

"You're right, Benny," Jessie said eagerly. She scrambled to her feet and threw her napkin in the trash. "Who wants to help me pick one out?"

"I do," Benny said, jumping up. He was happy they had a plan. He could hardly wait to catch the thief. Whoever stole the glove and the bat had taken Stockings. Benny was sure of that. And when Benny caught up with him — or her — there would be a lot of explaining to do!

CHAPTER 9

Setting a Trap

Half an hour later, they had made their choice. Benny picked out a baseball card with a picture of a famous player, Joe DiMaggio.

"I hope the thief falls for this," he whispered as Henry paid for the card.

"He will if we lay our trap carefully." Henry tucked the card into his jacket pocket.

"What are we going to do exactly?" Nicole asked. They moved away from the booth. She and Jessie were sharing a lemon ice, and it was melting quickly in the hot sun.

"We're going to pretend this is a birthday present for Coach Warren," Henry explained. "A *surprise* birthday present."

"And we'll make sure everyone on the team knows about the card," Jessie said, her face lighting up. "Then the thief will have a chance to steal it."

"We'll hide it someplace really obvious," Henry continued.

"And when the thief shows up, we'll be waiting," Violet finished.

"So he'll be the one who's in for a surprise!" Benny said.

"You said everyone on the *team* will know," Nicole pointed out. "What about Chuck?"

"We'll make sure he knows, too," Henry promised.

"I bet someone will come forward," Nicole offered.

Henry patted his pocket. "I think so, too. This card will lure them."

The Aldens spent a quiet Sunday with Grandfather, and returned to practice early on Monday morning. They were scheduled to play the Pirates the very next day.

"Remember to catch the ball with *two* hands, Violet," Chuck shouted as he crossed the field. "And Jessie, let's see some power when you swing the bat!"

Henry was hitting fly balls to Nicole. Chuck stood watching them for a few minutes. "That's much better, Nicole," he said.

"I've really been working hard on it," she answered. She knew she didn't dare take her eyes off the ball. Henry hit one to her again, and she made a perfect catch. She brushed her hair out of her eyes and grinned when Chuck applauded.

"Nice work, Nicole!"

"Thanks!" She knew she had played well, and she felt good.

As the day passed, the Aldens spread the word to everyone about the present they had bought for Coach Warren.

"It's a surprise," Benny said to Susan Miller at lunchtime, putting his finger over his lips.

"Don't worry, Benny," she told him. "I can keep a secret."

"Joe DiMaggio," Violet mouthed to Ann in the middle of practice as the two girls waited their turn at bat. Ann looked impressed.

"Don't drag your right foot, Jessie!" Coach Warren yelled. "Remember to plant it."

Ann waited until Jessie hit the ball with a sharp crack, and whispered back, "He's going to love it. When are you going to give it to him?"

"Right after tomorrow's game."

"I hope it's someplace safe," Ann said.

"It is," Violet assured her. "It's in the glove compartment of the van . . ."

Late that afternoon, the Aldens gathered on Grandfather's front porch with Michael and Nicole. Mrs. McGregor had made lemonade for everyone, and Benny was dangling his legs off the porch swing.

"How do you feel about tomorrow?" Michael asked Violet. "Any butterflies?"

Violet shook her head. "Not yet. I may get a few tomorrow morning though, when

we get to the field." She rubbed her arm. It was tired from throwing. "Right now, I can't even think about playing a single inning."

"I feel the same way," Jessie said. "I can't worry about the game right now. I'm still thinking about the baseball card that Henry planted in the glove compartment."

"You mean you're wondering who's going to steal it," Nicole offered.

Jessie nodded. "It's so hard to believe that the thief is someone on the team."

"It's even harder to believe that it could be Chuck," Violet said. She liked the friendly young man who had tried so hard to help her with her throwing. "I still can't figure out why he would want to hurt the Bears."

"We saw him with one of the Pirates team members in the store that day," Henry reminded her.

"That's true," Violet admitted.

"And he said that Hank Aaron was one of his favorite players," Michael suggested. "So he'd have a good reason for taking Jessie's glove."

"A lot of people would like to have that glove," Henry said. He looked at Benny. "Has Mr. Jackson ever said anything that sounded suspicious to you?"

Benny shook his head. "Just that he doesn't think girls should play baseball."

Nicole, Violet, and Jessie groaned. "There's something else funny about him," Benny said. "Remember the saltshaker on his workbench? He might have used that to make the new glove look old."

Everyone was quiet for a moment, lost in thought.

"He was fooling around with the lockers, too," Benny added. "He said that he was thinking of painting them, but they don't need it. Honest!"

"Why would he lie?" Violet asked softly.

"Unless he has something to hide," Jessie answered.

"Mrs. Sealy doesn't tell the truth either," Violet pointed out. "Remember that day we saw her in the store? She said she hadn't been to the dugout, but I don't think that's true. She had red mud all over her shoes."

"And she was on the field the day someone cut the cables on the van," Henry pointed out. "She brought brownies for Susan to pass around."

Benny nodded. "I remember them. They were good!"

Violet laughed and tousled her brother's hair. "You would remember something like that!"

"It sounded like she was plotting something with Mr. Jackson," Jessie said. "Remember when she said that the coach was going to get the 'surprise of his life'?"

"Well, there's nothing we can do but wait until tomorrow," Henry said. He leaned back in the white wicker chair. "If everything goes the way I think it will, we'll have our thief."

CHAPTER 10

Plenty of Surprises

"I think we have a shot at it," Jessie whispered to Violet the next day. "I think we can actually beat them!" They were playing against the Pirates on their own turf, and the Bears were in the lead.

Violet nodded, a little dazed. She couldn't believe how well everyone on the team was playing! She had surprised herself and made some good hits. All the long hours of practice had paid off, just as Chuck had said they would.

Benny was beaming as he rushed to bring

cold drinks to the players. It was so much fun being part of the team! It was nearly the end of the fifth inning, and the Bears were leading six to five. "We're going to win," he said under his breath. "We're the best!"

Michael took a big gulp of cool water and splashed some on his face. He felt hot, tired, and dirty, but he was having the time of his life. He was really happy that he and Nicole had met the Aldens. They had found such great friends.

"All we have to do is hold the lead," Coach Warren said to Henry and Chuck a little later. It was a close game, and Henry hoped the Bears would win.

The last inning passed in a blur, and when Nicole caught a fly ball for the last out, the Bears cheered. The Bears had won, eight to seven. "Hooray!" Jessie and Violet ran over to Nicole and threw their arms around her, jumping up and down. "Great catch!" Violet said.

Nicole beamed. "We really did it, didn't we?" She felt breathless and a little dizzy.

"We sure did!" Jessie cried.

Soon the rest of the team ran over, jumping up and down and cheering. They were very pleased with themselves. As they walked off the field, Benny said, "You should see Chuck. He's smiling from ear to ear!"

"So's Coach Warren," Michael offered. He lowered his voice. "When are we going to spring the trap?"

Henry moved closer. He knew that Michael was talking about the baseball card in the glove compartment. "We're going to start the party as soon as everyone cleans up."

Half an hour later, the Pirates had left the parking lot, and the Bears were milling around the field, sipping cold lemonade. Henry was just about to approach Coach Warren when a female voice rang out.

"Surprise, surprise!" Violet and Jessie turned to see Mrs. Sealy bearing down on them with a large birthday cake. "I hope Coach Warren can blow out all these candles," she said, teasing. She was balancing the cake carefully, and Jessie noticed that it was decorated to look like a baseball diamond.

Susan and her mother were right behind her, carrying napkins and paper plates.

"Did you know your aunt was planning this?" Violet asked quietly.

Susan looked a little embarrassed. "My aunt knew we were having a party to celebrate after the game, and she decided to bake a cake." She paused. "I'm surprised she knew it was the Coach's birthday. . . ."

Violet didn't say anything. Somehow, Mrs. Sealy always seemed to be in the middle of things.

A little bit later, after the cake had been cut, Violet wandered over to Henry. He was standing next to the van, his hand on the door handle. "Is the baseball card still there?" she said, glancing at the inside of the van.

Henry shook his head. "It's gone," he told her. "Just as I knew it would be."

"So the thief is right here!" It gave Violet a little chill to think that the thief was someone close by — someone so close she could almost reach out and touch him or her. She glanced around the field. Chuck was sitting next to Mr. Jackson in the dugout, eating cake, and Mrs. Sealy was talking to Coach Warren. Susan had been collecting signatures on a giant birthday card, and she made her way over to Violet and Henry.

"We can give this to the coach just as soon as you two sign it," she said. After Henry and Violet wrote their names, she headed for Coach Warren. Henry motioned for the rest of the Aldens to follow him.

"We'd like to wish you a happy birthday, Coach," Susan began. As Coach Warren took the card, Henry stepped forward.

"And we have a little present for you." To Violet's amazement, he took a plastic-wrapped baseball card out of his pocket.

"Why, thank you," Coach Warren said. His face lit up when he recognized Joe DiMaggio.

"How in the world . . ." Violet muttered.

Jessie edged closer. "That's the real card," she said in a low voice. "Henry substituted a fake one in the glove compartment to catch the thief."

"What do we do now?" Violet whispered.

"We spring the trap," Jessie said simply.

She moved quickly and stood between Susan and Coach Warren. "There's something you need to know, Coach," she began. "You know the series of thefts we've been having. . . ."

The coach nodded sadly. "I had hoped all that was behind us."

"I'm afraid it's not," Henry said firmly. "In fact, someone tried to steal your birthday present today. The Joe DiMaggio card."

The coach fingered the baseball card. "Are you sure?"

"I'm positive. That's why we set a trap and substituted a fake card in the glove compartment of the van." Everyone in the crowd was very still. Violet noticed that Chuck jammed his hands in his pockets, and Mr. Jackson looked worried. "And someone is holding the fake card right now. . . ."

"But who would do such a thing?" Susan blurted out. She looked at her aunt, who was fumbling with her pocketbook.

"I think it's you, Mrs. Sealy," Henry said quietly. "I saw you poking around the van earlier today. You had no reason to be there."

"This is ridiculous!" Mrs. Sealy blurted out. She clutched her pocketbook more firmly, and suddenly Violet realized that she had something to hide.

"How dare you accuse my sister!" Mrs. Miller said. "What would she want with a baseball card? Look, I'll prove it to you." Before anyone could stop her, she grabbed Mrs. Sealy's pocketbook and emptied the contents on a picnic table. "See, what did I tell you?" she said angrily. "Here's a hair-brush, some tissues, a change purse, and . . ." She paused, shaken. A plastic-wrapped baseball card lay squarely on the table. "Oh, no!" she gasped.

"And a baseball card," Henry said. He picked up the card and showed it to the group. "Joe DiMaggio. Except this one's not autographed."

Mrs. Miller looked astonished. "What's going on?" she asked, turning to her sister. Mrs. Sealy didn't answer, and stood with her arms folded across her chest. "Well, say something, Edna," Mrs. Miller persisted. "How did this end up in your purse?"

Mrs. Sealy hesitated for a moment, and then realized the game was up. "All right," she said. Her voice was low and angry. "I took the card."

"And that's not all you took, is it?" Jessie asked.

Mrs. Sealy shook her head. "I took some other things as well."

"But *why*?" Susan looked as if she was near tears. "Why would you do such a thing?" Violet felt sorry for her. It must be terrible to think that your own aunt would try to destroy your team.

"You know I wanted you to drop out of baseball," Mrs. Sealy began. "I thought if enough bad things happened, maybe you'd get disgusted and stop playing. Or maybe Coach would disband the Bears, I don't know . . ." Her voice trailed off. "I don't suppose this makes sense to you."

"No, it doesn't," Susan said. Her voice was shaky. "I love being on the team. And I never understood why you hate the game so much."

"Don't you see?" Mrs. Sealy took a step

toward Susan. "It takes time away from more important things. You could be a wonderful artist if you just spent more time painting. You're wasting your time on this . . . baseball field."

"Why didn't you just tell her how you felt?" Mrs. Miller asked.

Mrs. Sealy looked vaguely at her sister. "I tried to . . . I guess I never believed it would sink in. I thought this way would be better."

"You made a big mistake," Coach Warren said. "You've caused a lot of problems for us."

"I know. I see now that I was wrong." She paused. "I'm really sorry, Susan. You probably don't believe this, but I did it for you."

"But I wasn't giving up my painting," Susan said. Her voice was stronger now. "I'm still going to take lessons and paint every day in the off-season. I thought you knew that."

Mrs. Sealy shook her head and for a moment no one said anything.

"It's a big relief to know who did it," Chuck said.

"Did you take Jessie's mitt?" Benny demanded. "And then try to trick her with a fake one?"

"Yes, I took her mitt." Mrs. Sealy looked embarrassed. "But I don't know anything about a fake one."

"You don't?" Henry looked suspicious.

"She's telling the truth," Chuck said. "I felt so sorry for you, Jessie, that I tried to make you a new one. I guess I didn't fool anyone."

"*You* did?" asked Jessie. Chuck nodded, embarrassed.

"The new one still looked new," Jessie explained.

Benny turned to Mr. Jackson. "We were afraid maybe you were the one who switched gloves."

"Me?" Mr. Jackson looked surprised. "What made you think that?"

"You always keep a saltshaker in the dugout . . ."

"And salt can be used to make new leather look old," Violet finished for him.

Mr. Jackson laughed. "Well, I can explain the saltshaker to you. Hard-boiled eggs. I love 'em. Eat 'em all the time." He grinned. "But what's a hard-boiled egg without salt? Anyway, why would I want to hurt the team?"

"You said you didn't think girls should be on the team," said Benny.

"Well," Mr. Jackson said, "I'm beginning to realize I was wrong about that. Very wrong." He looked at Jessie and she smiled.

"But I saw you snooping around the lockers one day," Benny said. "You said they needed painting, but I knew they didn't."

"Oh, that." Mr. Jackson was embarrassed. "I have a little confession to make, Benny. I was trying to sneak Stockings back into your locker, but you caught me."

"Stockings! You found Stockings?" Benny was thrilled. He had his teddy bear back.

Mr. Jackson nodded. "My little granddaughter picked him up, Benny. But I was afraid everyone would think I'd stolen the other missing things."

"What about the bat?" Susan said suddenly. "How come I ended up with Ann's bat?"

"I'm responsible for that," Mrs. Sealy said. "I thought that if they suspected you of taking it, they'd throw you off the team."

"Edna! That was a *terrible* thing to do," Susan's mother said.

"I know." Mrs. Sealy stared at the ground. She looked very sad.

"Where's my glove?" Jessie spoke up. "I hope you didn't sell it!"

"It's in the trunk of my car," Mrs. Sealy said. "We can get it right now."

They walked silently to the parking lot, and Mrs. Sealy opened the trunk of her car and handed Jessie her glove.

Jessie thrust her hand inside it. She felt the little rough spot inside. This was the real glove from Aunt Jane!

"I think I better leave now," Mrs. Sealy said quietly. Everyone was watching her except Mrs. Miller, who had her arm around Susan.

"Wait, there's still something I don't understand," Jessie said. "What did you mean when you said that Coach Warren was in for the surprise of his life? I thought you and Mr. Jackson were plotting something."

"No, for once I wasn't plotting anything," Mrs. Sealy said. "Just a surprise birthday party."

"Something else is bothering me." Nicole stepped out of the crowd. "Did you cut the cables in the van that day?"

"Yes, I did." Mrs. Sealy's voice was so low Nicole could hardly hear her. "I wanted you to miss the first game of the season. I'll pay for the repairs."

"I suppose you took the keys to my van, too," Coach Warren said angrily.

Mrs. Sealy nodded.

"We thought *you* took them," Jessie said quietly to Chuck.

"And we thought you got lost on purpose, too," Michael added.

Chuck took off his baseball cap and ran his fingers through his hair. "No, I'm afraid I'm just lousy at directions."

"Who was that boy we saw you with in

the store?" Benny asked. "He plays for the Pirates."

"Oh, that's my little brother, Danny," Chuck said.

"You have a brother who plays baseball!" Jessie exclaimed. "Why didn't you tell us about him?"

"I was going to tell you about him when the season was over. I thought you might think it was kind of strange that he was playing for the other team." He paused for a moment. "You see, Danny joined the Pirates way before I started working for Coach Warren."

"We've certainly cleared up a lot of things," Henry said.

"I'm really sorry," Mrs. Sealy said in a small voice. "I just wanted Susan to quit the team." She looked so miserable, everyone felt sorry for her.

"Well, we all make mistakes," Coach Warren said gruffly. "Maybe we should just forget this one." Everyone was quiet while Mrs. Sealy started the car and pulled out of the parking lot.

"I'm glad that's over!" Chuck said, letting out a long breath.

"I'm glad that you figured out what was going on," Coach Warren said to the Aldens.

"I think we should try to put this behind us," Chuck said.

An hour later, the Aldens were celebrating with Michael and Nicole on the front porch of Grandfather's house. Benny was hugging Stockings tightly. Violet looked at her little brother and smiled.

"Things have a way of turning out all right, don't they?" she said. They had solved the mystery, and she had even hit a home run!

Jessie nodded. "Benny got Stockings back, and I got my autographed glove back."

"And we won the game!" Michael added. He remembered how exciting it had been.

"Do you think Susan will be okay?" Nicole asked. "I really feel sorry for her."

"I think she'll be fine," Henry said. "She knows her aunt made a big mistake, but it's all over with now." It was a warm evening, and Mrs. McGregor's garden was starting to bloom. "You know, we really did a good job today. We won the game and we solved another mystery."

"*Another* mystery?" Nicole asked curiously.

"Do you mean you've done this before?" Michael piped up.

Jessie laughed. "Many times."

"Wow," Nicole said softly. "Can you tell us about them?"

"Sure," Benny told her. "But it'll take a long time!"

THE MYSTERY OF THE HIDDEN BEACH

created by
GERTRUDE CHANDLER WARNER

Illustrated by Charles Tang

ALBERT WHITMAN & Company
Morton Grove, Illinois

The Mystery of the Hidden Beach
created by Gertrude Chandler Warner;
illustrated by Charles Tang.

ISBN 10: 0-8075-5404-9
ISBN 13: 978-0-8075-5404-3

For more information about Albert Whitman & Company,
visit our web site at www.albertwhitman.com.

Contents

CHAPTER 1

Welcome to Camp Coral

"Are we almost there?" Violet asked eagerly. She was wedged in the front seat between Grandfather and Henry as the rental car sped along the Overseas Highway toward Key West, Florida.

"We just passed Key Largo," Grandfather told her, "so we have another couple of hours to go."

"And we have a lot more Keys to go," Jessie piped up from the back seat. "Sugarloaf Key, Eagle Key, Big Pine Key . . ." She reeled off the names from a map that Soo Lee had spread across her lap.

"I hope we'll be at Camp Coral in time for dinner," said Benny, who was six. He loved to eat.

"The names are so pretty," Soo Lee said. She stared out the window at the turquoise water that inched right up to the narrow ribbon of highway. The silvery blue-green Atlantic Ocean was on the left, and the Gulf of Mexico was on the right.

"I'm glad you came with us, Soo Lee," Violet said.

"So am I." Soo Lee was a seven-year-old Korean girl who had been adopted by Joe and Alice Alden, the Boxcar children's aunt and uncle. She was looking forward to sharing adventures with her new cousins.

"I think we'll see a lot of the islands and keys at Camp Coral," Jessie assured her. "They have fourteen boats, and we'll be on the water every day." Jessie, who was twelve, was the most organized of the four

Boxcar children, and she had read the camp handbook from cover to cover.

"I'll be on the water, too," Grandfather said. "Jake loves to fish and I expect we'll be out catching blue marlin and snapper for dinner." He had already explained to the children that he would be visiting his friend on Upper Matecumbe Key while they were at camp for a week.

"I bet you'll have fun, Grandfather," Violet said, resting her hand on Grandfather's shoulder. Ten-year-old Violet Alden was a shy, sensitive child, who was very attached to her grandfather. She remembered the days when she and her sister and brothers were orphans, living in a boxcar, and Grandfather had found them and given them a real home.

It was late afternoon when Henry, who was fourteen, spotted a small green sign. "That's it," he said excitedly. "Turn here for Camp Coral, Grandfather." They left the highway and headed down a narrow dirt road bordered by a tropical jungle of mangrove trees and palms. A pair of white herons streaked across the sky, and a small deer darted across the road into a thicket.

A few minutes later, they arrived at a collection of white stucco buildings nestled at the edge of a dazzling blue ocean. Two giant palms framed a nautical-looking sign: WELCOME TO CAMP CORAL. A piece of fishermen's net was draped over one corner, and a thick coil of rope formed the words.

"We're here!" Benny shouted. As soon as Grandfather pulled into the parking lot, Benny scrambled out of the car. Jessie and Soo Lee were right behind him.

"It's just like I pictured it," Violet said, turning to help unload the luggage from the trunk. A group of campers were paddling kayaks close to the shore, and two young girls walked by in wet suits. They were carrying goggles and flippers, and one of them waved to her.

"Why are they dressed like that?" Benny asked curiously.

"They're probably going snorkeling," Grandfather told him. "Or maybe even scuba diving. They teach both here at the camp."

"And we teach a lot of other fun things," a young woman said, walking up to them. She was wearing cut-off shorts and a red T-shirt with the word STAFF printed on it. "I'm Melanie, the activity director," she said, sticking out her hand to Grandfather. "And you must be the Aldens."

Grandfather shook Melanie's hand and introduced everyone. Then a loud bark made Melanie turn in surprise. "Oops," she said, reaching down to pat a friendly-looking collie. "I forgot to introduce Bingo. He's the camp mascot."

"We have a dog back home," Benny said. "His name is Watch."

Melanie smiled at him. "Then I'll give you a special assignment, Benny. You can give Bingo his doggie treat every day after dinner. Would you like that?"

"You bet!"

"Now, after you say your good-byes, I'll take you to your cabins." She bent down to pick up one of the duffel bags lying next to the car.

"Good-bye, children," Grandfather said, embracing each of the children in a big hug. "Have a wonderful time, and I'll see you next week."

"Good-bye, Grandfather," Jessie said, somewhat sadly.

"We'll miss you!" Violet added.

Grandfather started the engine and the children waved until the blue car had rounded a turn in the dirt road and was out of sight.

"Ready, everyone?" Melanie asked. "The boys' cabins are on the right, and the girls' are straight ahead." Everyone trooped after her as she headed for a long white building and tapped on the door. A moment later, they stepped into a cheerful room lined with bunk beds. A braided rug was on the floor and fresh muslin curtains billowed at the windows. "Nobody's here at the moment. I guess everyone's in class or doing an activity."

"In class?" Benny said, surprised. "I thought this was a camp."

Melanie laughed. "Sometimes you have to learn things before you can do them." She helped Henry and Benny unload their backpacks on two empty beds, and then pointed to the window. "Take a look outside."

Violet pushed aside the curtains and saw a young boy wind-surfing over the glittering blue water. He balanced himself confidently on the board, handling the sails smoothly as he skimmed along. "Oh, it looks like fun. Can we do that?"

"Yes, you can, but first you have to learn how to do it safely," Melanie promised. "That's what I meant by going to class. You begin by practicing on dry land."

"On dry land?" Benny wrinkled his nose. "I bet you don't get very far that way."

"No, that's true. But if you fall, you only

fall a few inches onto the sand." She reached down to ruffle Benny's hair. "We have a special wind-surfing simulator, Benny, and you feel just like you're on the water. It's a great way to practice."

"With none of the risks," Henry offered.

"Exactly." Melanie moved to the door. "Now if you boys want to get settled, I'll take the girls to their cabin."

A few minutes later, Soo Lee, Jessie, and Violet were unpacking their clothes in a spotless cabin almost identical to the boys'.

Jessie sat down cross-legged on her bed, studying a thick booklet. "Wow, have you seen this activity list? They have classes in everything you can think of — marine science, scuba diving, snorkeling, canoeing . . ."

"Oh, this looks good," Violet said, peering over her shoulder. "We can sign up to visit the site of an underwater shipwreck. Maybe we'll find some sunken treasure."

"I think that's for the advanced students

who know scuba diving," Jessie said. "We'll probably have to start with snorkeling and see how it goes." She started to say more, but a hearty knock at the door interrupted her.

"Hey, have you seen this!" Benny barreled into the room, waving the activity booklet. "Henry and I have already picked out our favorites," he announced. "Henry wants to learn underwater photography, and I want to learn ichy . . . ichy . . . how do you say this word?" He turned to his brother who was right behind him.

"Ichthyology," Henry told him.

"The study of fish," Jessie murmured.

"That's right," Benny said, bouncing on her bed. "I want to learn all about sharks." He thumbed eagerly through the book. "Everything in here looks good. We can swim over a coral reef, we can learn all about dolphins and whales. . . ." He scrunched his forehead in thought. "I don't know what to do first!"

"I think I can help you with that decision,"

Melanie said. The activity director was standing in the doorway, checking her watch. "In just three minutes, the bell is going to ring for dinner. How about if I walk you over to the dining hall?"

"Dinner?" Benny scrambled off the bed so fast he almost tumbled on the floor. "Let's go!"

Violet and Jessie laughed at the surprised look on Melanie's face.

"You just named his favorite activity of all," Jessie explained.

CHAPTER 2

A Night on the Water

"We have about thirty campers right now," Melanie explained as they moved through the cafeteria line. Benny had piled his plate high with spaghetti and meatballs and was reaching for a slice of Key lime pie. "Most of them are kids, but we have a few adult guests, too."

"I guess grown-ups like to learn about the ocean, just like we do," said Soo Lee thoughtfully.

"That's right." Melanie paused and

scanned the room. "You see that tall man with the beard sitting over by the window? That's Nick Simon. He's a marine biologist. That means he studies animals and plants that live in the ocean."

"Could we meet him?" Benny asked eagerly. "I have a zillion questions I'd like to ask him about fish."

"Sure," Melanie said, making her way past long tables filled with tanned campers in T-shirts and shorts, all enjoying delicious dinners. "Follow me."

A few minutes later, the Aldens were sitting down at a table with Nick Simon and a couple named Hilary and Joshua Slade, who ran a charter sailing company. Nick Simon was nice, but the Slades weren't very friendly. It seemed as if they'd rather be sitting alone.

A thin young woman approached the table. "Is there room for one more?" she asked. She spoke rapidly as if she were a little nervous.

"Of course, Katherine," Melanie said.

"We would be delighted if you'd join us." She turned to the Aldens. "This is Katherine Kelly. She's an underwater photographer."

"That must be fun," Jessie said, biting into a piece of garlic bread.

Katherine Kelly shrugged. "Sometimes. I'm here to take some pictures of coral formations for an article in a nature magazine."

"I guess you know that we have a long stretch of coral here in the Keys," Melanie explained to the Aldens. "The reef runs a hundred and twenty-eight miles." She turned to Benny. "You'll get a chance to see some of it this week when we take a glass-bottom boat ride."

"Will I get to see all those fish I read about?" he asked Henry. Grandfather had bought Benny a book on tropical fish before they left home, and they had read some of it every night before bed.

"I'm sure you will see lots of them,"

Henry answered. "Which one is your favorite?"

"Oh, the car-wash fish," Benny said promptly.

"The car-wash fish?" Melanie laughed. "I've never heard of that one, and I've lived down here all my life."

"That's just a name I made up," Benny said. "It reminds me of a car wash. The fish all line up, and this really pretty blue fish cleans the tiny parasites off their bodies." He turned to Nick Simon. "What's the real name? I forget."

Nick Simon looked uncomfortable. "It's . . . well, that must be . . ." He scratched his chin, and looked helplessly at Melanie. "I can't seem to come up with the name of that fish."

"You must mean the blue angel fish," Melanie said slowly. Henry noticed that she looked a little taken aback. Nick Simon was a marine biologist. Surely he had heard of a blue angel fish?

"And I want to collect seashells," Benny announced. "Lots of them."

"Me too," Violet added. "I like the ones that are pink and white. You can hold them up to your ear."

"Oh, those are conch shells," Katherine Kelly said. "You'd better not touch them. You can get slapped with a five-hundred-dollar fine for removing them." She sounded annoyed.

"Five hundred dollars just for picking up a seashell?" Henry asked. He looked doubtful.

"She's right," Melanie assured him. "We have signs posted around Camp Coral to remind you. You're not allowed to take any conch shells from the camp." Her voice was very serious. "And you shouldn't even touch the coral because the bacteria on your hand can kill it."

"But my hands are clean!" Benny said. He held up his hands to show her, smiling proudly.

"I'm sure they are, Benny, but the slightest

human touch can destroy an entire stand of coral that took thousands of years to grow," Melanie insisted.

After dinner, the Aldens changed into bathing suits and joined Hilary and Joshua Slade and some other campers at the edge of the water. A boat was anchored at the shore, and Melanie was handing out plastic pails to everyone.

"What are we doing?" Soo Lee asked. "Are we going fishing?"

"Sort of. Each of you is going to collect specimens to keep in your aquarium. Just fill your pail with sea water, and step on the boat. I'll explain more once we get going," Melanie said.

"But I don't even have an aquarium," Benny protested.

"Oh, yes, you do." Melanie grinned. "You have your very own aquarium with your name on it in the ocean studies room. I checked it this morning. Each of you has one."

"My own aquarium!" Benny was excited. "What's in it?"

"Well, nothing but salt water just yet. But I bet you'll collect lots of exciting fish tonight."

Violet looked doubtful. "What if we pick the wrong fish?" she asked. "What if they eat each other?"

"Don't worry. I'll be here to help you." Melanie helped the campers into the boat. Then she cast off the thick rope that anchored it and signaled to a young man to start the engine.

They moved swiftly over the crystal water until Melanie signaled to stop the engine. "Let's stop. It's shallow here," she said, jumping overboard. The water rose just past her knees. "You can collect some really pretty sponges, and there are plenty of algae and sea fans."

"Ooh, there's something spiky down there," Violet said, peering nervously into the water.

"That's a sea urchin. You can take him. He'll do fine in your pail," Melanie assured her.

When everyone had gathered sponges and sea grass, they all got back in the pontoon boat and then headed for another shallow area.

"Oh, I see what I want," Soo Lee said as soon as the boat stopped. They were near the edge of a mangrove-lined shoreline. "It's a starfish!" she said, jumping into the water to collect her prize.

"I found a horseshoe crab," Henry said, plunging his hand underwater.

Benny had just used a net to capture a rainbow parrot fish when he noticed Joshua Slade grab something from the sandy sea bottom. He watched in amazement as the charter captain tucked it under his shirt. Was he really stuffing a fish inside his clothes? Why didn't he drop it in his bucket of salt water?

Before he could say anything, Violet an-

nounced that she had found a live conch, and with Melanie's permission, she placed it carefully in her pail.

"I thought we weren't allowed to take those," Hilary Slade objected.

"We return all the specimens to the ocean once we've studied them in the aquarium," Melanie reassured her. "This conch will never leave Camp Coral. It will go right back where it came from."

After the sun set, the group headed back to camp, where Melanie helped them set up their tanks. "You have a little free time now," Melanie said. "But I'd suggest you turn in early. We have a big day tomorrow."

"Your aquarium is beautiful," Soo Lee said a few minutes later. Violet had just arranged a sea fan against the rear wall of her five-gallon tank. Her prized conch was settled on a pile of red algae and sea grass.

"Thanks. Melanie said he eats algae, so I'm hoping he'll get hungry and come out."

"Did Melanie tell you what a conch looks like?" Henry asked her. "Like a big brown tongue!"

After everyone had finished arranging their tanks, they emptied their pails of sea water and stacked them neatly in the store-room. The Aldens left the classroom build-ing and stepped into the balmy night air. There was a full moon, and a soft breeze rustled through the stately palms that fringed the grounds. A few of the staff members were building a fire on the beach, and someone was strumming a guitar.

"Do you want to join them on the beach?" Henry asked.

Benny gave an enormous yawn and Violet looked at Henry. "I think we should turn in. Benny looks like he's going to fall asleep standing up."

"I am not!" Benny said indignantly. He hated to go to bed because he never wanted to miss a moment's fun. He clapped his hand over his mouth just as he started to yawn again.

"Time to say good night," Henry said, steering his little brother toward the boys' cabin.

An hour later, Benny was tucked into bed, his mind filled with memories of the ride out to the grass flats. Collecting fish had been a lot of fun, and he was very proud of his beautiful parrot fish. Suddenly he frowned. He really should tell Henry about Joshua Slade hiding a fish inside his shirt! That was the strangest thing he had ever seen. Unless, of course, it wasn't a fish . . . but what else could it be? Before Benny could answer his own question, he drifted off to sleep.

Meanwhile, in the girls' cabin, Violet sat up in bed and whispered, "Soo Lee, are you awake?"

"I am now," Soo Lee answered with a laugh from the neighboring bed. "What's wrong?"

"I just remembered something. Did you notice if I turned on the filter in my aquarium?"

"I'm pretty sure that you did," Jessie said sleepily. "Didn't it make kind of a whooshing noise?"

"I don't know. I'm just not sure. If the filter isn't on, there won't be enough oxygen in the water." She bit her lip. "I don't know what to do."

"There's only one thing to do," Jessie said. "If you don't go back and check, you're going to worry about it all night."

"We'll come with you," Soo Lee offered. She reached for her robe.

Minutes later, the three girls made their way along the winding path to the classroom building. All the lights were out, but Violet was relieved to find the side door was unlocked. When Violet found the light switch, she hurried to the aquarium.

"See, I told you everything was okay," Jessie called to her. "I can see the water bubbling from here."

"Everything's not okay," Violet said in a trembly voice.

"What's wrong?" Jessie asked as she and Soo Lee hurried to Violet's side. Violet pointed wordlessly to her tank.

"Oh, no!" Soo Lee said. "Your beautiful conch shell is gone!"

CHAPTER 3

A Very Special Island

The next morning, Violet reported the theft to Melanie at breakfast. The counselor's expression was grim as she noted the time that the girls had visited the classroom building.

"Somebody really worked fast," she said. "I closed up half an hour earlier." She pushed her plate aside, her food untouched. "I must have forgotten to lock that side door, though," she said, shaking her head in disbelief.

"Why so glum? The scrambled eggs can't be that bad," Nick Simon joked, sliding into the seat next to her. He had a plate of pancakes and a steaming cup of coffee.

"Somebody stole Violet's conch shell," Benny said. "They took it right out of her aquarium last night."

"Really?" Nick's eyes darkened.

"I'll have to report it to the authorities," Melanie said quietly. "Nothing like this has ever happened before."

Jessie looked around the crowded cafeteria. It was hard to believe, but the person who stole the conch shell could be eating breakfast in the dining hall at that very moment!

Melanie noticed Violet's downcast expression. "How about if I take all of you on an outing this morning? I can't promise you another conch shell, but I'll show you a beautiful spot."

Violet brightened. "Where are we going?" she asked.

"To my own hidden beach." Melanie lowered her voice. "It's a very special place and no one else knows about it."

"You own your own beach?" Soo Lee asked.

"Not exactly." Melanie smiled. "But when I'm all alone there, sitting under a palm tree, I can pretend that I do! It's my favorite place to be."

Half an hour later, the Aldens were skimming over the water in a small powerboat. The water shimmered in the bright sunlight as Melanie maneuvered the craft toward a tiny island.

"We're going to an island!" Benny exclaimed.

"There are hundreds of islands in the Keys," Melanie explained. "A lot of them don't even have names. I discovered this one a few years ago. And ever since, it's been my special place."

When they reached the island, Melanie cut the motor and pointed to a dense thicket of mangrove trees. "I'm afraid we have to take

a little hike to get to my favorite spot." She handed out large beach towels with the Camp Coral insignia. "Be sure to wrap these around your waists. The undergrowth is pretty thick here, and I don't want you to get all scratched up."

A few minutes later, after cutting through a narrow, twisting path, they found themselves on a beautiful stretch of deserted beach. Everyone peeled off their beach towels and plunked down happily on the soft white sand.

"Are you sure no one else knows about this place?" Violet asked.

"As far as I know, it's all mine," Melanie told her. "Most of the staff members find their own little getaway spots. Sometimes you just want to be by yourself."

"I think somebody else has discovered your private island," Henry told her. He reached over and yanked a shiny object out of the sand.

"A chisel?" Jessie said in surprise. "That's

strange. Why would anyone bring a chisel to the beach?"

Melanie shook her head. "I can't imagine." She looked at the bright yellow handle. "It's not from Camp Coral. We stamp all our tools with a double C."

"Melanie, can we go swimming?" Benny asked. The bright Florida sun was making him hot.

"Sure, or how about wading? There's a really nice coral bed here and we can take a few pictures, if you like." Melanie reached into her duffel bag and pulled out a small camera and some goggles. "Who wants to be the photographer?"

"I do." Violet said, jumping to her feet. "I've never seen an underwater camera before."

"I'll show you how to use it. It's really easy," Melanie told her.

Everyone waded out into the warm water, and Melanie led them to a patch of brightly colored coral.

"I thought you had to go way out in the ocean to find coral," Henry said.

Melanie nodded. "To get to the barrier reef, you do. That's where we're going tomorrow. But this kind of coral — shallow bay coral — is found in knee-deep water." She handed Violet the camera and quickly explained how to use it.

"Remember, don't touch anything," Jessie said to Benny. He was staring at a clump of coral just a foot away.

Melanie handed out goggles to everyone. "You really have to put your face in the water to get the full effect of the colors. Take a look. That's golf ball coral right next to your foot. And there's a nice chunk of finger coral over on the right."

"Something strange is going on down here," Violet said, startled. She pulled her head out of the water, still clutching the camera. "I tried to get a picture of some coral and it moved!"

Melanie peered into the clear blue water. "Oh, that's rose coral, Violet. Whenever it gets covered up with sand, it spits out a little jet of water. That's how it turns itself right side up."

They waded around for another half hour, being careful not to disturb the coral in any way. Violet took a lot of pictures, and Benny was excited when he spotted a strange-looking fish swimming past him.

"Hey!" he yelled to Melanie. "What's that?" He pointed to a small translucent disk bobbing on the water.

"A jellyfish," she replied.

"Are you sure it's a fish? It's got something green trapped inside it," Jessie said. "It looks like a plant."

"It is a plant. Some jellyfish carry their food with them," Melanie explained.

"Just like we put granola bars in our backpacks," Benny piped up.

"Exactly."

After they'd eaten a tasty lunch, Melanie took the Aldens back to camp. There they piled into a van with some other campers to visit Key West.

Jessie admired the beautiful old Victorian houses, with tropical plants spilling out of their window boxes. The streets were lined with stately palms and banyan trees, and the air smelled like flowers.

They drove toward Mallory Square on a street lined with shops. A vendor was cutting open fresh coconuts and selling them to a group of children, who raised the rough brown shells to their lips.

"What are they doing?" Violet asked, puzzled.

"They're sipping fresh coconut milk," Melanie told her. "It's delicious. If we have time, we'll stop and buy some on the way back."

After Melanie parked the van, they wandered through an open air market that was filled with tourists. The hot afternoon sun made everyone move slowly. Violet watched as a man made a basket out of palm fronds. Soo Lee bought a delicate bracelet with the money Grandfather had given each of them for souvenirs. Benny looked over a selection of shells, and finally chose a chalky white sand dollar.

After Benny paid for his prize, he looked up in surprise. "Look, there's Nick Simon from camp." He pointed to a tall bearded man who was deep in conversation with another man. "I want to show him my new sand dollar."

Melanie watched as Benny scampered over to the marine biologist. "That's funny," she said.

"What's that?" Jessie was picking through a pile of tiny brass rings.

"I asked Nick Simon if he'd like to ride into Key West with us today, but he told me he had too much to do back at camp," she said with a shrug. "I guess he changed his mind."

"Nick Simon liked my sand dollar!" Benny said, running back to the group. "And guess what — he told me his friend is a real fisherman!"

Henry glanced over at Nick Simon's friend, a pale, sandy-haired man in his early thirties. The two men quickly turned their backs and headed down to the docks. "He sure doesn't look like a fisherman," Henry said. "Look how pale he is. He looks like he never goes in the sun."

"Everybody else around here is tan," Jessie said. She shrugged. "Maybe he's the captain of the fishing boat, and he stays inside while other people fish."

"Maybe," Melanie said, but she didn't look convinced.

"Where shall we go now?" Violet asked. She sat under a date tree and unfolded her Key West map. "We can go to the Key West Aquarium, or we can see Mel Fisher's Museum."

"What kind of museum is it?" Benny was peering over her shoulder.

"It has all kinds of sunken treasure," Melanie explained. "Mel Fisher discovered the *Atocha*, a ship that sank hundreds of years ago. It was filled with gold bars, and lots of emeralds and jewelry."

"But the aquarium is interesting, too," Violet pointed out. "It has loads of fish, Benny, and I've heard they even let you touch an eel."

"Wow!" Benny exclaimed. He was stumped. Fish or sunken treasure — how could he ever choose? He turned to Melanie. "Could we do both?" he asked. "We could go to the aquarium right now and then come back to Key West another day to visit the museum."

"That's fine with me," Melanie said with a smile. "I can see that you don't want to miss anything."

Jessie laughed as Benny hopped up and down. No one had more energy than her little brother!

CHAPTER 4

Petting a Shark

"So that's why they call them parrot fish!" Violet said excitedly a few minutes later. Melanie and the Aldens were peering into a large tank at the Key West Aquarium where a dazzling fish zipped through the crystal-clear water. It was brightly colored and had a beak almost like a bird's.

"Parrot fish use their beaks to scrape algae off the coral," Melanie explained. "Unfortunately, they can leave some pretty bad scars on the reef."

Jessie steered them to another large tank, where a young man was giving a lecture. He lifted something dark and wriggly out of the tank, and held it up carefully in front of the visitors. "This is a nurse shark," the man explained. "Would anyone here like to pet her?"

Benny's eyes lit up. "Can I?" When the man nodded, Benny stepped closer and carefully stroked the shark's side. Then he drew his hand back in surprise. "It feels just like sandpaper!"

"Will it bite?" Violet asked, waiting her turn to touch the shark.

"No, nurse sharks are completely harmless. They're very gentle," Melanie told the Aldens."

After they learned about porcupine puffers and sea cucumbers, the guide lifted a large conch shell out of the tank.

"That's just like the one you found," Jessie whispered to Violet.

"I know," Violet said, admiring the pink and white spiral shell. She wondered who had broken into the classroom building that night, and if the thief would ever be caught. She hoped so.

"This is the horse conch," the guide was saying. "Maybe he'll come out for us." He waited until something large and brown slithered out of the shell.

"There he is!" Benny leaned forward for a closer look.

Everyone watched as the conch inched across the guide's hand, and then lumbered slowly back into his shell. "The conch is a very interesting marine animal. He eats red algae and moves one mile in twenty-four hours."

"Wow! That's pretty slow," Henry pointed out.

Benny giggled. "Not if you're carrying your house on your back!" He suddenly spied a pretty blue fish in another tank. "Look," he said, tugging at Melanie's hand.

"That's the fish I told you about. The car-wash fish."

Melanie nodded. "The blue angel fish," she said, reading the label on the tank. "You have a good memory, Benny," she told him. "He cleans up the other fish by eating parasites off them."

The same fish that Nick Simon had never heard of, Henry thought.

Later that night over a delicious dinner of fried chicken and mashed potatoes, Benny was telling the whole table about his visit to the aquarium.

"We even saw a barracuda," he said proudly. "He was swimming really fast underwater."

Nick Simon smiled at him politely. "They can be very dangerous," he pointed out. "Just remember to get out of the water if you see one headed your way," he added jokingly.

"Or better yet, don't wear any jewelry while you're swimming," Melanie said, pointing to a thin silver chain around Nick Simon's neck.

The marine biologist looked at her blankly. It was clear to everyone that he had no idea what she was talking about. Violet finally turned to Melanie. "What do you mean?"

Melanie shrugged. "Everyone knows that barracuda are attracted to things that are shiny. If they see a flash of silver in the water — like a chain — they think it's something to eat. You see, their favorite food is a type of little silvery fish." She paused and stared right at Nick Simon. "But then, you know that."

"Yes, of course," Nick said quickly. He looked a little embarrassed.

"I definitely don't want to be dinner for a fish!" Benny exclaimed and everyone laughed.

"Don't worry, Benny," Melanie reassured him. "We'll make sure that you're not."

When dinner was over, the Aldens decided to check on their aquariums. Jessie had picked up a few pretty, colorful shells at the market and she wanted to add them to the tank.

They were working in the classroom building, when suddenly Benny remembered something. He tugged at Henry's wrist. "Something really strange happened the night we went out in the pontoon boat." He quickly told everyone about seeing Joshua Slade pluck something out of the ocean and hide it in his shirt.

"He didn't put it into his bucket the way he was supposed to," Benny said, confused. "He stuffed it right here." He pointed to his chest.

"What was it?" Soo Lee asked.

"It couldn't have been a live fish," Jessie pointed out, sensibly. "It would have been wriggling."

"Maybe it was a conch shell," Violet offered, thinking of her own shell.

"No, that would be too big to fit under his shirt," Henry said.

"Maybe it was a really pretty shell and he didn't want the rest of us to see it." Jessie

suggested as she carefully added a sea fan to her tank.

"But what did he do with it?" Soo Lee asked. She glanced at the tank that Joshua Slade shared with his wife. It was almost empty except for a few wisps of sea grass and a couple of angel fish. "He didn't put it in his tank."

On the way back to their cabins, they noticed Ned, one of the counselors, guiding a boat toward the dock. The craft was filled with campers, and Violet remembered that a night expedition was scheduled that evening. Usually boats weren't taken out at night, but this was a special occasion.

"Let's see what they got," Benny said eagerly. "Melanie said you can find some nice fish that only come out at night."

They were almost at the water's edge when they spotted Joshua Slade strolling by. He seemed lost in thought and was startled when Ned tossed him a line from the boat. "Would you mind tying that for us?" Ned asked.

"Sure, I . . . I'll be glad to." Joshua Slade

looked helplessly at the line in his hand, and looped it uncertainly around the piling. "There you go," he said brightly, and hurried off.

When Ned leaped nimbly off the boat, he looked at the line and shook his head. "What kind of knot is this?" Henry heard him mutter. "The guy doesn't know how to tie up a boat!"

"Did you hear that?" Henry asked as soon as they were out of earshot. They were walking down the winding path that led to the cabins.

Jessie nodded. "Mr. Slade is supposed to run a sailing company, but he doesn't know how to tie a knot?" She paused. "That doesn't make any sense at all."

"A lot of things don't make sense," Violet added. "Mr. Simon is supposed to be a marine biologist, but he didn't know that barracuda like to eat little silvery fish. Melanie had to explain it to him."

"And he didn't know about the car-wash fish," Benny reminded her.

"That's right," Henry agreed. "And now look at Mr. Slade. I never heard of a sailor who couldn't tie a simple knot!"

They were at the girls' cabin, and Violet stopped outside the door. "I'm beginning to think that Melanie is the only person around here who really knows everything she's supposed to."

"She sure does," Benny said enthusiastically. "I like her a lot!"

"We all do," Jessie said. "Time to turn in, little brother. We have a big day tomorrow."

"I know," Benny said, dancing down the path to the boys' cabin excitedly. "Windsurfing at eight, sailing at ten, and snorkeling at two."

"Aren't you forgetting something?" Henry said teasingly.

Benny thought a moment, then shook his head. "I don't think so."

"Breakfast at seven!"

Benny grinned and rubbed his stomach. "I could never forget that!"

* * *

The next morning, Benny raced through the cafeteria line so he could be the first one to try the wind-surfing simulator. It was a wide flat board, mounted on a giant spring. If you stepped on the board and shifted your weight, you felt just like you were bouncing back and forth over the waves. "It seems funny surfing on dry land," he said, as he hopped on the machine.

"You won't think it's so funny if you land on your bottom," Melanie told him. "The beach sand is nice and cushiony. It will break your fall."

"I won't fall," Benny said.

"Maybe not." Melanie positioned his feet on the board. "But nine out of ten people do. It's a lot harder than it looks."

For the next ten minutes, Benny practiced balancing on the board and working the sails. "Wow, this is hard," he said, tugging the sail in one direction, then another. "But it must be lots of fun when you finally try it in the ocean."

"It's a lot of fun," Melanie promised. "But we have to make sure you do it safely on land first. And once you're on the water, you'll be wearing a life jacket. That's in case you tumble into the water," she said. "Not that I think you will."

Each of the Aldens took turns, and Jessie caught the hang of it right away. "When can we try the real thing?" she asked, her face flushed with excitement.

"I know you think you're ready to go right now, but you still need some more practice," Melanie said firmly. "I want everybody out here for half an hour every day, because you can't try it in the ocean until you master it on land."

"Oh no!" Benny groaned.

"It's not easy," Melanie pointed out. "But if you practice hard, we'll try to get you on the water, Benny."

CHAPTER 5

Someone's Stealing Coral!

The following afternoon, Melanie invited the Aldens back to her favorite beach for a delicious picnic lunch. They had spent the morning learning all about dolphins.

"I asked the cook to pack some special lunches for us," she said, pointing to a large cooler. "Sandwiches, fruit, and fresh lemonade." She looked at Benny. "Plus a dozen homemade brownies," she said, knowing his eyes would light up.

"Let's go!" Benny said, racing down to the dock.

"What did you learn about dolphins this morning?" Melanie asked half an hour later. They were sprawled on beach towels, enjoying their lunch.

"Our teacher said they're really smart," Benny said. "They talk to each other with special sounds, and they like to play." He paused, munching on his sandwich. "And they love to eat. They eat about twenty pounds of fish a day!"

Violet laughed. "I guess you've finally met your match, Benny."

"Dolphins always look happy," Soo Lee added. "It looks like they are smiling."

"But they only look that way because their mouths turn up at the corners," Henry said. "The instructor told us that they get bored and unhappy sometimes, just like people. That's why it's not fair to keep them caged up in little pools to do tricks. They enjoy living with other dolphins in the ocean."

After lunch, Melanie and Henry wandered down to the water's edge. Melanie scuffed her toe on a seashell and looked down in surprise. "That's funny. It looks like someone else has been here." She stared at a set of footprints in the hard-packed sand along the shoreline.

Soo Lee ran across the beach to join them. "Can I wade out and look at the coral?" she asked.

"Sure," Melanie said good-naturedly. She looked worried, though, and Henry knew she was upset that someone had been on her island.

Henry and Melanie were ambling along the shore when a sudden shout from Soo Lee made them turn in alarm.

"What's wrong?" Henry shaded his eyes from the bright sun.

"It's gone!" Soo Lee said, peering into the water. "The coral!"

"Oh no," Melanie said, dropping to her knees in the shallow water. "It looks like someone's taken a sledge hammer to it!"

Benny, Jessie, and Violet raced down to the water to see the damage. The coral bed had truly been destroyed. The beautiful branches had been hacked off, and all that remained was a jagged base on the ocean floor.

Melanie turned to them with tears in her eyes. "We need to go back to camp right away and report this."

"Of course," Jessie said. The children helped Melanie gather up the picnic things. They hurried back to the powerboat and Melanie quickly started the engine. As they skimmed over the water, everyone was silent except Benny.

"I don't understand," he said. "Why would anyone want to ruin anything so beautiful?"

"For money." Melanie's voice was tight as she steered the boat skillfully over the gentle, lapping waves. "Coral is worth a fortune, and there's not much of it left."

"But how did anyone even know about that particular coral bed?" Henry asked.

"You said you've been coming to the island for years, and it's always been deserted."

"I don't know," Melanie admitted. "But that's something I need to tell the Coast Guard."

"The Coast Guard?" Benny's eyes were wide.

"Stealing coral is a serious crime," Melanie told him. "We'll call the authorities as soon as we hit camp. I bet they'll start an investigation right away."

An hour later, the Aldens found themselves being interviewed by Mr. Larson, a friendly man from the local Coast Guard Station.

"Can you describe the coral bed?" he asked the children. "I already have Melanie's statement, but you might have something to add."

"It was a very large bed, and really pretty," Jessie began. "I know there was rose coral and finger coral, because Melanie pointed it out to us. . . ."

"Wait a minute!" Violet blurted out. "We can do more than describe it — we can show you a picture of it!" She turned to Melanie. "Remember, you showed me how to use that underwater camera."

"So I did," Melanie said, looking relieved. "Now we'll have an exact record of the bed."

"Where's your camera?" Mr. Larson asked.

"It's in my cabin," Melanie said. "I can get it for you."

"Did someone mention pictures?" Katherine Kelly asked. She had walked into the lodge so quietly no one had heard her. "Maybe I can help. I'm an underwater photographer."

"I don't think so, Katherine," Melanie said. She looked at Mr. Larson to see if he would volunteer any information, but he shook his head very slightly. Apparently he wasn't ready to discuss the case with anyone else just yet.

Katherine Kelly waited awkwardly for a

moment, and then said brusquely, "Well, I'd better get going then. I've got a lot of work to do this afternoon."

As she turned to leave, Benny noticed a series of thin red scratches on Katherine Kelly's calves. "What happened to your legs?" he blurted out.

The photographer glanced down in embarrassment. "Oh, it's nothing," she said, touching the fiery red marks. "I was playing with Horace, and I guess he got carried away." She managed a thin smile before hurrying from the room.

"Horace?" Violet said in amazement. She had met the large orange tabby when they had first arrived at camp. "He's the world's friendliest cat. He never scratches anyone."

"Not even Bingo the dog," Benny piped up.

On her way back with the camera for Mr. Larson, Violet bumped into Joshua Slade.

"Taking some pictures?" he asked.

Violet nodded. "I have a roll ready to be developed."

"What did you photograph?" He seemed unusually talkative, and Violet wondered why he was so interested.

"Some tropical fish, some pretty sea grass. . . ." She thought it was better not to mention the coral or the ongoing investigation.

"Oh, is that all . . . see you later!" Joshua walked abruptly away.

What did he mean by that? Violet wondered. What had he thought she was going to say?

After Violet handed over the film to Mr. Larson, she and Melanie strolled back to the beach to practice wind-surfing. The rest of the Aldens had decided to spend the afternoon learning about underwater shipwrecks. "I know you feel really sad about the coral bed," Violet said.

"I do," Melanie admitted. "It was very special to me." She bent down to adjust the wind-surfer. "I just hope they find the thief before any more coral is lost. It takes thousands of years to grow, and it can never be replaced."

She helped Violet position her feet on the small board, and showed her how to move the sails. "Do you remember what I taught you?"

"I think so." Violet kept her balance and tugged at the sails, just as if she were on the ocean. But her mind was elsewhere. Joshua Slade was friendly one minute, and unfriendly the next. Why? Katherine Kelly was covered with scratches and blamed it on the cat. But the cat was friendly and never scratched anyone. And Nick Simon didn't seem to know a thing about marine biology. There were so many mysteries at Camp Coral.

"Violet, hold the sails with more force. You're letting them get too slack!" Melanie said.

"Sorry," Violet muttered and tightened her grip.

"That's much better," Melanie said approvingly. "You'll be out in the waves in no time."

"Thanks." Violet smiled at the counselor, still thinking. None of the little mysteries could compare to the big mystery they were all facing. Who was stealing coral? Violet would have some free time after dinner that evening, and she knew exactly how she was going to spend it. It was time for an Alden family conference. Maybe all four of them — and Soo Lee, of course — could catch the thief and solve the mystery.

CHAPTER 6

Benny Finds an Unusual Coin

The camp was quiet when the Aldens gathered at a picnic table down by the dock later that evening. Many of the campers used their free time to read and relax in their cabins, while others worked on their craft projects like painting, macrame and pottery.

Violet told everyone her suspicions of Katherine Kelly, Joshua Slade, and Nick Simon. When she finished, no one said anything for a moment.

"Does anyone have any ideas?" she asked, watching as Benny skimmed a flat rock over the water.

Henry looked thoughtful. "I wonder if there could be a logical explanation for some of the things we've noticed."

"There's something else funny about Joshua Slade," Benny said. "Remember, I saw him stuff a fish in his shirt."

Jessie laughed. "We're not sure it was a fish, Benny, but you're right," she said. "It sounds like he was hiding something that day we were all out collecting specimens together."

"That's true," Soo Lee agreed. "But what about Katherine Kelly? I can't believe that Horace really scratched her legs."

"You're right, that does seem strange," Jessie offered. "But why would she lie about it?" Suddenly she remembered the first day they had visited Melanie's island. They had wrapped beach towels around their legs to protect themselves from the dense underbrush. "The mangrove trees!" she exclaimed.

"If Katherine Kelly scratched her legs when she was stealing coral on Melanie's island, she wouldn't want anyone to know about it. She had to explain the scratches somehow, so she blamed Horace."

"But how would she get to the island?" Henry asked. "Only counselors are allowed to use the boats."

"She could go out very quietly at night when everyone was asleep," Soo Lee suggested.

"I saw lights on the water one night!" Benny said, turning back to the group. "Do you think that's a clue?"

Jessie smiled. Benny always loved to solve a mystery. "There are probably a lot of boats on the water at night, Benny, and they all have lights." When she saw the disappointed look on his face, she added, "That could be a good clue, though, Benny. We'll have to remember that."

Henry was leaning against a palm tree, staring out at the darkening sky. "You know, I just thought of something else important.

Remember that chisel I found the first day at the island? That could have been left there by the thief."

"That's a good point," Jessie said. "We need to mention that to Mr. Larson from the Coast Guard. I'm sure he'll be back tomorrow — "

Suddenly a slim figure stepped out from the shadows. "A lovely evening, isn't it?" Hilary Slade smiled at Benny and skimmed a stone across the water, just as he had done a few minutes earlier. "I used to love to do this, too, when I was a kid," she said in a friendly way.

Had she been standing there all the time? Violet wondered. Had she been eavesdropping on their conversation?

Henry was puzzled too. Why was she making such an effort to be nice? She rarely bothered to talk to the children at dinner and had only spoken a few words to them during their whole time at camp.

Hilary turned her attention to Soo Lee. "That's beautiful," she said, touching the bright yellow jute. "It's macrame, isn't it? How did you ever learn to do that?"

"I'm taking a craft class," Soo Lee explained. "It's not very hard," she added, holding up the bright yellow band. "I picked an easy pattern. It has only two different kinds of knots."

"Two kinds of knots?" Hilary looked impressed. "I could never do that. I'm all thumbs."

"No, it's easy, really," Soo Lee insisted. She handed her the strip of macrame. "All you have to know is a square knot and a half-hitch." She pronounced these new words carefully.

"Never heard of them," Hilary said with a laugh. "I guess I'll take your word for it, though."

Soo Lee looked surprised. "But my teacher said they are the same knots sailors use." she said. "Don't you use them on your boats?"

"Oh, well . . ." Hilary's face was flushed

and she looked embarrassed. "I leave all that up to my husband." She quickly thrust the macrame into Soo Lee's hands. "Well," she said briskly, "look how dark the sky is getting. I must be getting back to the cabin. See you tomorrow!" Before anyone could say a word, she turned away and hurried down the path.

"She certainly wanted to leave in a hurry," Violet said.

"I think she didn't want us to know that she didn't recognize those sailing knots," Jessie added.

"So now there are four people who are suspects," Soo Lee said.

"Four?" Benny asked. "I thought we had three — Joshua and Hilary Slade, and Katherine Kelly."

"Don't forget about Nick Simon," Henry said grimly. "Every time anyone asks him a question about fish, he seems to draw a blank."

"And he's supposed to be a marine biologist!" Jessie exclaimed.

"And there's something else about him," Henry said. "He seemed worried when we spotted him in Key West talking to that fisherman friend of his."

"Who might not be a fisherman at all." Jessie stood up. "Remember how pale he was?"

Henry nodded. "I don't think he's telling the truth about his friend, but I can't imagine why he would lie."

Benny yawned, and Jessie took him by the hand. "I think we should all get a good night's sleep, and maybe we can figure out some answers tomorrow."

When Benny started to get up, he noticed an old coin wedged between the wooden slats of the picnic table.

"Look!" said Benny, showing the coin to Henry and Jessie. "I'm going to keep this!" The coin was dented and uneven around the edges, but Benny didn't mind. He loved to collect things, and he stuck it in his pocket.

The next morning at breakfast, the Aldens sat at a long table by the window, discussing the mystery. They stopped talking abruptly

when Joshua and Hilary Slade joined them.

"Good morning!" Hilary said cheerily to the Aldens.

Everyone greeted her politely, but Henry was more suspicious than ever. Why was she being so friendly?

"What are your plans for the day?" Joshua asked.

"We're going on a glass-bottom boat ride over the coral reef this morning," Jessie told him. "And then we're going back to Key West in the afternoon to visit a treasure museum."

"A treasure museum! That certainly sounds like fun," Hilary said. "Wouldn't it be just wonderful to find some real buried treasure?"

"That's what Mel Fisher did," Henry told her. "He and his wife discovered a famous ship called the *Atocha*. It was a Spanish galleon that went down in a hurricane in the 1600's off the coast of Florida."

"I read about it," Jessie said. "It had been lying on the ocean floor all that time, and was full of treasure — gold bars, coins, and jewels. People had been looking for it for years, but it was Mel Fisher who finally found it."

"Did he bring it up?" Benny asked excitedly. "Can we go see it?"

"The *Atocha* is still on the ocean floor, but he brought up all the treasure. He has a lot of it on display in his museum," Henry told his brother.

"And that's where we're going today!" Benny said. "Yippee!"

"You seem to be really interested in treasure," Joshua said.

"I am! I collect coins," Benny said proudly. "I found a really interesting one last night."

"Really? What's it like?" Joshua stopped eating, his fork in midair.

"Well, it's really old, and it's hard to read what it says on it." He paused, surprised at their interest.

"Do you have it with you?" Hilary asked sharply.

"No, it's back in my room." Benny looked a little uncertain. Hilary suddenly seemed irritated with him.

"What else did you notice about the coin?" her husband persisted.

Benny shrugged. "It's uneven around the edges." He grinned. "That's what I like about it. That's what makes it special."

"Does it have any markings on it?" Hilary leaned close to him, her eyes piercing. "Try to remember."

Benny scrunched his forehead in thought.

"It has a coat of arms on it, doesn't it?" Violet said.

"A coat of arms!" Hilary was so excited she jiggled her cup, and her coffee flooded the saucer. She pushed it away and looked at her husband. "I don't feel very hungry. Why don't we head back to the cabin?"

"Good idea." Joshua pushed back his chair. "See you later," he said briefly to the children.

"Those two are acting really suspicious lately," Jessie said quietly to the others. "I think we should keep an eye on them."

Jessie nodded and swallowed a forkful of pancakes. "So do I. Right now, there are four suspects, and the Slades are at the top of the list."

CHAPTER 7

A Trip to the Coral Reef

"You're going to see some beautiful coral out at the reef," Melanie said, as they boarded a glass-bottom boat later that morning. They had driven into Key West after breakfast and were taking their seats on the upper deck of a large white boat called the *Fury*.

"And fish, too?" Benny asked. He had already learned to identify several kinds of tropical fish, and wanted to see more.

Melanie laughed. "Over six hundred varieties. That's enough to satisfy any fish lover!"

As soon as the boat got under way, Melanie asked the children what they knew about the coral reef.

"I know it's over a hundred miles long," Violet said. "And it runs just offshore of the Florida Keys."

"That's right," Melanie agreed.

"Why don't we have any coral reefs up near Greenfield?" Benny asked.

"Because the reef is made up of coral polyps, and they need warm water to survive. They die if you put them in water that's cooler than seventy degrees."

An hour later, they dropped anchor over a large coral bed, and everyone went below to the observation deck. "Wow, now I see why they call this a glass-bottom boat!" Benny dashed along the narrow walkways dividing glass panels that revealed the ocean floor.

"The fish are so close we could touch

them," Violet said, watching as a midnight-blue parrot fish glided by.

"I think this fish had too much to eat," Benny said, dropping to his knees to get a better look. He pointed to a large tan fish that looked almost round.

"That's a Southern puffer," Melanie said. "He's not really fat, Benny. He sucks in a bellyfull of water and makes himself look three times as big. That way, he scares off other fish who might bother him."

Jessie admired some beautiful elkhorn, staghorn, and branch coral, and Melanie reminded her that they grow only two or three inches a year.

"It's seems funny that coral is actually alive," Violet pointed out.

"But it's true. The coral reef is constantly growing new colonies of polyps on top of the skeletons of older ones. Coral can live for centuries. The reef is thousands of years old."

As Melanie talked about the reef, Henry's

mind went back to the coral theft on the island. Would the Coast Guard be able to catch the thief? he wondered. He went over the list of suspects that they had come up with, and felt confused. That was the whole problem, he decided. There were plenty of suspects, but no real clues. And worst of all, no proof!

After lunch, the group headed to the Mel Fisher Museum to see the riches of the famous Spanish ship, the *Atocha*. Benny was thrilled to touch a genuine gold bar, and Jessie admired a beautiful belt studded with rubies and diamonds. "Do you know dolphins were trained to bring up some of the emeralds from the wreck?" a museum guide asked.

"Emeralds? Why would dolphins be interested in emeralds?" Violet asked, puzzled.

"Because we rewarded them with their favorite treat — mackerel!"

* * *

That evening, at bedtime, Benny thought about his own treasure — the bent coin he had found at the dock. He had seen a picture of Mel Fisher wearing a gold coin on a chain around his neck. Benny wanted to do the same thing. "Henry, can you drill a hole in my coin tomorrow?"

"Sure, Benny, I'll be glad to." Henry tucked the covers around his little brother, and within minutes, both boys fell fast asleep.

It was nearly midnight when Benny awoke with a start. He heard a faint rustling noise, but he couldn't pinpoint exactly where it was coming from. And he was too scared to open his eyes.

"Henry, is that you?" he whispered. There was no answer. He strained to listen, as goosebumps rose on his arms. Should he scramble out of bed and wake his brother? He decided to wait a couple of more minutes.

He was completely awake now, and he knew he wasn't imagining what he heard.

Something was brushing against the lamp-shade on his night table. Something was jiggling the brush and comb on his dresser top. Something was bumping into his bed.

"Henry?" Benny said softly, his voice trembling.

Just then he heard the door creak open. Benny lay very still, listening. But the cabin was quiet now.

Benny couldn't stay still another minute. He jumped out of bed and raced across the room to flip on the light switch.

"What's going on?" Henry sat straight up in bed, rubbing his eyes.

The cabin was flooded with light, and Benny pointed to the door. It was open!

"Someone was in here," Benny stammered. "Someone was here, in our cabin."

"Are you sure?"

"I'm positive." He jumped back in bed and pulled his knees up to his chest. Even though the danger was over, he still felt scared, and his teeth were chattering.

Henry crossed the floor and checked the solid pine door. "It could have been the wind," he said hesitantly. "But this is a pretty heavy door."

"It's not just the door!" Benny protested. "Something was moving all around the room. I heard it!" He looked around the room nervously. "Maybe it was a . . . ghost." He lowered his voice to a whisper. "Do you think that's possible?"

Henry peered around the open door and laughed. "Here's your ghost." Bingo darted into the room, barking happily.

"Bingo?" Benny said doubtfully. "Do you think that's what I heard?"

"It must have been." Henry reached down to pat the furry collie who immediately jumped onto the bed. "Maybe he was lonely and just wanted some company."

Benny wasn't convinced. "But how did he get the door open? And what was he doing under my bed?"

Henry watched as Benny scrambled under the bed and dragged out the cookie tin.

The top was half off, but his coin was safe. "Why would he be sniffing around a metal box?"

Henry shrugged. "I don't know. Maybe he remembered when it held cookies." Bingo jumped down and began nosing the tin. "See? It probably still smells like food to him."

"If you say so," Benny said, climbing back into bed.

Henry ushered Bingo out of the cabin and closed the door firmly behind him. "Let's get some sleep," he said, returning to his own bed.

"Okay, but I'm going to leave my light on," Benny said in a little voice. "Just in case."

The next morning, Henry went to the craft room after breakfast to drill a hole in Benny's coin. "How's that?" Henry said, holding it up. Soo Lee had given Benny a piece of jute to use as a cord, and Benny fastened the coin around his neck.

"Now I look like a real treasure hunter!" he said proudly.

Meanwhile, Jessie, Violet, and Soo Lee were sitting in the darkroom, watching as Melanie explained how to develop black-and-white photographs.

"After you put the prints in the final bath," she said, "you carefully lift them out of the solution with tongs and hang them to dry." She pointed to a long line that ran the length of the room. "You might want to take a look at the work that my advanced students have done. There's some beautiful underwater photography there."

"Oh, look at this one," Soo Lee said, pointing to a pretty sunset scene.

"That one was done by a professional," Melanie said. "Katherine Kelly took that photograph."

Violet walked over to the picture and stared at it for several seconds.

"What's the matter?" Jessie asked, noticing the serious expression on her face. "Don't you like it?"

"Oh, yes, it's beautiful," Violet said. "But . . ."

"But what?" Soo Lee interrupted.

Violet shrugged. "I don't know. There's something about that picture. It looks so familiar."

"Maybe you saw it on a postcard," Jessie teased her. "You know, sunset, water, palm trees. Everywhere you look in Key West, you see the same scene."

Violet shook her head. "No, it's something else. It's more than that." Everyone left to have lunch then, but Violet couldn't resist taking a last look at the photograph. Why was the picture so disturbing? Where had she seen it before? She knew it was going to bother her until she remembered. She would just have to think.

Jessie came back to drag her out of the darkroom. "Hey, we're going to be last in the cafeteria line, if we don't get a move on. And they're having pizza today. They might run out!"

"I'm coming," Violet said reluctantly.

Jessie looked at the picture and shrugged. She wondered why Violet was so troubled by it. Jessie nudged her sister playfully. "Come on, Violet. You worry too much. Let's go eat!"

CHAPTER 8

The Thief Returns!

At lunch that day, Joshua Slade hurried to catch up with the children as they started to move through the cafeteria line.

"How are you doing today, Benny?" he asked cheerfully. "Did you have fun in Key West?"

"We saw some treasure from a shipwreck, and I got to hold a real gold bar," Benny told him. His eyes were fixed on the goodies in front of him. Should he have a hot dog or a grilled cheese sandwich?

Again, Henry wondered why the man was being so friendly. And something else made him suspicious. Joshua was leaning forward, craning his neck to get a view of Benny's neck. Why?

A moment later, the mystery was solved. "That's an interesting coin you're wearing, Benny. Is that the one you found down by the dock?"

Benny nodded, helping himself to a big bowl of chopped mangoes and papayas.

"Think I could look at it?" Joshua added. "I've always been interested in coins."

"Sure," Benny said absently. He held the coin away from his neck so Joshua could see it. "Henry drilled a hole in it for me. See, it's got a really nice design on it, and you can still read a few letters on the top — "

Joshua's eyes narrowed as he inspected the coin, and then he turned away, irritated. "Yeah, it's a great coin, kid." His voice was harsh. "See you later." He dropped his empty tray back in the rack and left the cafeteria abruptly.

Violet nudged Jessie. "What was that all about?"

"I don't know." Jessie glanced at Benny, who was reaching for a glass of milk. At least he didn't seem bothered by Joshua's rudeness.

"Joshua Slade acts very strange, don't you think?" Violet asked.

Jessie nodded. "Very strange. One minute he's friendly, and the next minute, he acts as if he doesn't like us."

As they ate lunch, Benny said he wanted to practice on the wind-surfing simulator that day.

"He's done a good job," Henry said to the girls. "Melanie said that we'll be able to go into the water soon."

"Shallow water," Melanie said, slipping into a seat beside him. "With life preservers."

Jessie nodded. At Camp Coral, safety always came first. "Have you heard anything

new from the Coast Guard?" she asked
Melanie.

"They don't have any leads yet," Melanie
said regretfully. "I told Mr. Larson we'd all
be on the look-out, but there's not much else
we can do." She paused, and her eyes
skimmed the crowded cafeteria. "Until the
thief strikes again, of course."

"You think the thief will come back?"
Benny's eyes were as big as saucers. He
really wanted to catch the coral thief before
they left camp. What a story this would be
to tell Grandfather! They had solved dozens
of mysteries in the past, and this might be
the most exciting one of all.

"I'm sure he will," Melanie said grimly.
"I just saw a new report on how much
money people are getting for a boatload of
coral. I bet the thief is greedy enough to try
again."

"You think it's someone at camp, don't
you?" Soo Lee asked. She had noticed the
way Melanie had looked around the room
moments earlier.

Melanie nodded. "It seems impossible, but yes, I do." She waved to a shy-looking young girl with a ponytail. "Excuse me," she said, pushing her chair back. "That's a new camper and she's feeling a little home-sick."

Everyone turned in early that night after a long, busy day out in the sun. Around midnight, Jessie awoke with a start. She heard a strange noise outside and sat straight up in bed, listening intently. *Putt-putt. Putt-putt.* "Someone's starting up a boat out there," she said softly. She knew it was against the camp's rules to take boats out at night.

She quickly woke her sister and Soo Lee. "Do you hear that noise?" she said, pointing to the open window. The noise had grown a little fainter, but could still be recognized.

"It's a boat," Soo Lee said sleepily.

"It sounds strange," Violet added. "It seems to skip a beat sometimes."

"Why is somebody out on the water at this time of night?" Jessie asked, pulling on her shorts.

"What are you doing?" Violet turned on the lamp next to her.

"Well, we can't just sit here listening," Jessie said impatiently. "It could be the coral thief. He could be out there stealing coral right this minute."

"Oh, no, you must be right," Violet said, scrambling out of bed. She struggled into a pair of jeans and reached for a flashlight. "Get dressed fast, Soo Lee. We need to do some investigating!"

"Let's get Henry and Benny," Soo Lee suggested.

"We'll have to hurry," Jessie said.

"I'm ready." Soo Lee had pulled on a pair of khaki shorts and a T-shirt.

They woke up the boys, and everyone hurried down the pathway to the dock. It was a balmy night, and a full moon made the bay look silvery. Even though it was warm, Jessie shivered a little.

"I think we're too late," Violet said when they reached the dock. The children stood silently, peering into the darkness. A bird called softly, but otherwise everything was still. The boat was nowhere in sight, and the engine noise had disappeared.

"Do you suppose he's sitting out there in the dark, and he cut the motor?" Henry asked. "Maybe he can see us standing here, and he's waiting for us to go back inside."

Jessie stared as hard as she could. There was absolutely no movement, no sign of anyone. "No," she said, disappointed. "I'm afraid there's nothing out there. He's just . . . gone."

"If only we had been quicker," Violet said.

"Maybe we can find some clues, just by looking around," Jessie suggested.

"Looking around here?" Benny asked doubtfully.

"You never know what may turn up. Let's walk along the dock before we give up," Jessie insisted.

They walked along the row of boats, each lost in thought.

"Look at that!" Soo Lee said suddenly. She pointed to an empty berth.

"Number six." Jessie grabbed Soo Lee's arm in excitement. "That's where that little white powerboat is always docked."

"So whoever is out on the water took it," Violet said.

"Unless they had permission to be out at night," Jessie said.

"I don't think so," Henry said. "Only the counselors have keys to the boats, and they don't go out at nighttime."

"Well, at least we learned something important tonight," Jessie said, as they headed back to their cabins. "We know someone was out on the water, and we know which boat they used. Tomorrow, we'll tell Melanie and decide what to do next."

CHAPTER 9

To Catch a Thief!

The next morning, the girls spotted Melanie in the cafeteria and told her about the mysterious boat they had heard during the night. "I'll have to report this," Melanie said. She looked very serious. "No one is allowed to take boats out at night — not even counselors." She paused, stirring her coffee. "And you're sure berth number six was vacant?"

Soo Lee nodded. "Yes."

"Well, whoever took the boat out returned

it," Melanie said. "I was down at the docks half an hour ago, and all the berths were filled."

Benny came racing into the cafeteria just then, followed by Henry. "We're getting closer and closer to the thief," Benny said.

"Maybe not," Violet said doubtfully. "Maybe he got everything he wanted last night, and he won't show up again."

After breakfast, the Aldens decided to take a quick look at the docks. Maybe they could find a clue they had missed the night before. As they strolled along the docks, Benny stared hard at the powerboat docked in berth number six. It looked absolutely normal — white fiberglass finish, a wood-grain dashboard, blue vinyl seats. . . .

Suddenly he stopped dead in his tracks. There was something shiny lying on one of the seats. What was it? It was so small it would fit in the palm of his hand, and it glinted in the morning sun. He tugged urgently on Henry's arm. "Look at the seat!"

he said in a hushed voice. "What is it? Can you reach it?"

Henry used one hand to steady himself and quickly stepped inside the boat. He scooped up the bright object and was back on the dock in a flash.

"What is it?" Benny was nearly jumping up and down in excitement.

"A clue," Henry said, opening his hand. Everyone crowded around to look at a small gold cigarette lighter. It was initialed with the letters NS. "Probably a very important clue."

"NS," Violet said thoughtfully. She and Jessie exchanged a look. "Nick Simon!" they said in unison.

"I think he's just moved to the top of our list of suspects," Benny said.

That evening, the counselors took some of the campers to Bird Island for a cookout. The Aldens rode in a large boat, and Melanie rowed across the bay in a rowboat.

"That looks like fun," Benny said, watching as Melanie smoothly guided the rowboat through the water.

"You certainly did a good job on the wind-surfing simulator," Jessie said. "Grandfather will be proud of you. We'll be seeing him tomorrow, you know."

"Tomorrow?"

"We've been here a whole week," Violet reminded him. "The time went fast because we've been doing so much."

"And learning so many new things," Soo Lee added.

"I wish we could stay longer," Benny said. "I never got to use the real wind-surfer. The kind that goes in the water."

Violet put her arm around him. "Maybe next time, Benny."

After dinner, everyone sang songs and toasted marshmallows around a campfire. Soo Lee had never tasted marshmallows before, and Benny showed her how to thread them on a stick and hold them over the flames.

"Mmmm!" she said when she'd tried her first toasted marshmallow. "This is great!" Violet felt a little sad because she knew she would miss the camp, and especially Melanie, who had become a good friend. And worst of all, they had never solved the mystery of the missing coral!

"Are you thinking the same thing I am?" Jessie said quietly. She had caught the look on her sister's face as she stared into the fire.

Violet nodded. "Probably. I've been thinking about the coral thief — who he is, what he's planning to do next. This is the first time we've come up against a mystery we couldn't solve."

Jessie sighed. "I know. All we can do is hope that the thief slips up somehow, and Melanie catches him after we leave."

A little later, the counselors suggested a hike around the island, but the Aldens decided to stay at the campfire. The sun had already set in a blaze of fiery orange, and the night air was soft and balmy.

"It's so peaceful here," Jessie said. "I want

to sit and watch the stars come out one by one."

"I want to watch the moonlight," Violet said. "It looks so pretty when it shines on the water."

"And I want to watch the campfire," Benny said. "We still have another whole package of marshmallows left!"

Everyone laughed, and the group began hiking along the shore, leaving the Aldens alone.

Darkness spread across the island very quickly, and half an hour later, Benny was startled to see a flashing light on the water. It was at the far end of the island, but he could see it clearly, twinkling in the distance. He stood up, curious, and then he heard a familiar sound. *Putt-putt. Putt-putt.*

"There's that boat again," Violet said in a hushed voice. "I know it!"

Henry and the girls scrambled to their feet. "How can you be so sure?" Henry asked.

"Because it's the same boat we heard a couple of nights ago," she insisted.

"Don't all powerboats sound alike?" Henry asked.

"This one's different," Violet said, shaking her head. "It skips a *putt* every now and then. I know it's the same one we heard before. Boat number six."

"You're right," Henry agreed. "Melanie said that the boat has a bad transmission, and that's why it skips every so often."

"What can we do?" Jessie asked eagerly.

Suddenly the *putt-putt* sound stopped, and the Aldens stood motionless, straining to hear.

"Why has the noise stopped?" Benny whispered.

"I don't know — " Violet started to say, and then stopped. All at once she realized what was going on. "Oh, no!" she cried. "The thief has docked the boat. What if he's going to steal more coral?"

"We have to get Melanie and the other

counselors," Henry said. "And we need to move fast."

"They've been gone for a while," Jessie said. "How will we find them?"

"We'll have to split up," Henry said. "Violet, you and I will take the rowboat to the other end of the island. At least we'll know what's going on, and we may even get a look at the thief."

"Soo Lee and I can try to find the campers," Jessie said.

"Don't walk along the shoreline. It will take too long," Henry pointed out.

"We'll cut through the woods instead," Soo Lee said quickly. She scrambled to her feet, glad that she had worn long pants and sturdy shoes.

"Hey," Benny said. "How about me?"

"You're coming with us," Henry said, grabbing his hand.

"Good — there are three life jackets inside," Violet said when they reached the rowboat a couple of minutes later. They quickly put them on, and Henry helped Violet and Benny into the rear seat. Then he lowered himself into the middle seat and took up the oars.

When they had almost reached the shore at the other end of the island, Benny heard a sharp sound. "What's that?" he asked.

"I bet the thief is using a hammer on the coral bed," Henry said in disgust. "We'll have to hurry."

They docked the rowboat as quietly as they could and crept cautiously along the hard-packed sand. The beach was very dark, but suddenly they saw a light dancing at the edge of the water, just a few yards away.

"That light's moving all by itself!" Benny said in a shaky voice.

"No, there's a person holding it," Violet said. She grabbed Benny's hand and held it tightly. "Someone's coming out of the water and he's all dressed in black. That's why you can't see him."

"He's wearing a wetsuit," Henry whispered. They inched a little closer. Violet noticed that the person was slim, and carrying a big chunk of coral. A snorkel mask covered most of his face.

"Who is it?" Benny asked, edging close to Violet.

She shook her head. "I can't tell yet. Let's see what he does."

They watched as the dark figure lifted the coral into a powerboat docked nearby and went back into the water.

"He's after more coral!" Violet said angrily. "We have to stop him!"

"I know," Henry said, "but we need help. Can you stay here and try to get a look at his face? I'm going to take the rowboat and find the others."

"Be quick," Benny said.

"Don't worry, I will," Henry assured them.

He darted back to the rowboat, just as the thief emerged from the water. After dropping another load of coral in the powerboat, the figure in the wet suit stopped to rest for a moment.

"What's he doing now?" Benny whispered.

"I don't know — " Violet started to say, and then stopped. The figure had pulled off his snorkel mask, and Violet nearly gasped in surprise. It was Katherine Kelly!

She started to inch backward, still clutching Benny by the hand, when he gave a sharp yelp of pain.

"Oh, Benny," Violet said. She didn't want Katherine to see them.

"I'm sorry," he said in a little voice. "I stepped on a shell."

Katherine's head swung around at the sound, but before she could spot them, Violet ran into the woods and pulled Benny behind a giant banyan tree.

Suddenly an arm appeared out of the darkness. It grabbed Violet by the shoulder and she almost screamed.

"It's okay," a calm voice said. "It's only me." When the man stepped closer, she recognized his face.

"Nick Simon?" she asked doubtfully.

What was he doing in the woods at night?

"There's nothing to be afraid of," Nick said. Violet wasn't sure if she could believe him.

"What's going on?" Henry's voice boomed out.

"We're over here!" Violet called out. Her brother was at her side in a second.

"I was just stepping into the boat when I heard Benny cry out," Henry said. Then he looked at Nick. "What are you doing here?"

"I'm here for the same reason you are. To catch the coral thief."

Henry hesitated. Was Nick telling the truth? Up until now, he had been one of the main suspects.

"He's not the thief!" Benny blurted out. "It's Katherine Kelly. We saw her!"

"Where is she?" Nick asked.

"She's down at the beach," Violet said.

"That's all I need to know," Nick said. He took a walkie-talkie out of his pocket and spoke a few words. When he finished talking, he smiled at the children. "They'll pick her up in a few minutes. We have officers all over the island."

"Officers?" Jessie said in surprise. "You're with the police?"

"Detective Nick Simon," he answered, pulling out his badge. "I've been working undercover for months, trying to get a lead on the thief. But you're the ones who really solved the crime," he told them. "I knew it was someone at Camp Coral, but I couldn't figure out who."

"Neither could we," Henry said. "We even suspected you."

"Are you sure the police will get there in time?" Violet said worriedly. "All she has to do is jump in the powerboat and get away."

"Not without this, she won't." Henry held up a thin wire. "She can't get far with her spark plugs disconnected."

Nick laughed. "You'd make good detectives."

CHAPTER 10

The Mystery Is Solved!

"That about wraps it up, Nick," a pale man with sandy hair said a few minutes later. He was standing at the edge of the shore, watching as another officer handcuffed Katherine Kelly, and helped her into a police patrol boat.

"I know you!" Benny said. "I met you with Nick in Key West. He said you were a fisherman."

Nick laughed. "This is Officer Adams, Benny. I'm afraid I had to tell a little white lie. I couldn't explain that we're both undercover investigators."

"What's going to happen now?" Henry asked. He glanced at Katherine Kelly, who glared back at him.

"It's an airtight case." Officer Adams pointed to a group of men in Coast Guard uniforms who were carefully placing the stolen coral in clear plastic bags. "We've got eyewitnesses, we've got the stolen coral, and we've got the tools she used."

"It sounds like you caught her in the act," Nick said.

Officer Adams nodded. "We did. She had just dumped another load in her boat. It's funny, but she couldn't get the engine started. That was a lucky break for us."

Nick laughed as Henry held up the wire. "It was more than just a lucky break. Henry disconnected her spark plugs. She'd be miles away by now, without the help of my young friends."

Jessie and Soo Lee appeared just then,

followed by a group of counselors and campers.

"What's going on?" Jessie asked, and then gasped as she spotted Katherine Kelly in handcuffs. "She was the one?" she whispered.

"That's right," Benny said excitedly. "We caught her stealing the coral and we recognized her when she took her face mask off. And then — we had to run into the woods! It was scary!"

"I'm glad you're okay," Jessie said, giving him a quick hug.

"Someone better fill me in," Melanie said, coming up behind Jessie. She was out of breath. "We heard the noise and ran all the way back from the other side of the island."

Nick smiled. "Well, the bottom line is that the kids solved the crime for us. Without them, Katherine might have made one last haul, and then disappeared for good."

"But I don't understand," Jessie said. She

turned to Nick. "You're not really a marine biologist?"

Violet laughed. "He's a police officer, but it's a long story."

"I have a lot of questions, too," Melanie said. "How about if we all go back to Camp Coral and discuss it?"

Half an hour later, everyone met at the picnic tables down by the dock at the camp. The other officers had left the island, but Nick stayed behind to talk about the case. Melanie lit some tiki lamps, and the campers and counselors gathered close to ask questions.

"Was she really an underwater photographer?" Soo Lee asked.

"Yes, she was a real photographer. Her work has been featured in some big magazines." Nick paused. "I guess she just decided she could make more money from stealing coral."

"It was the picture! That's what made me wonder!" Violet blurted out. Everyone turned to look at her. "Katherine took a really pretty picture of a sunset and we saw it hanging to dry in the darkroom."

"I remember how much that picture bothered you," Jessie said. "But I never understood why."

"I didn't either — until now." She turned to Melanie. "There was something about the rock, and the sunset that looked so familiar. I realized that I had seen that exact same view before — from your private island!"

"So the only way Katherine could have gotten that picture was if she had been standing in the same spot we were," Jessie said slowly. "She probably discovered the big coral bed that day and decided to chop away at it."

"It will take hundreds of years to grow back," Melanie said sadly.

"Don't feel bad, Melanie," Violet said, edging close to her. "At least she'll never be able to do it again."

"When did you first suspect her?" A male voice came from the back of the crowd.

Henry turned to see Joshua Slade raising his hand.

"Right from the start," Nick answered. "But I suspected a lot of people. You and your wife, for example."

Hilary Slade laughed nervously. "Surely you didn't suspect us."

"I certainly did. You two don't know much about sailing for a couple who are supposed to run a charter business."

"That's right!" Soo Lee agreed. "You didn't even recognize a square knot when I showed you my macrame piece."

"And you stuffed a fish inside your shirt!" Benny piped up. "I saw you that night we were out collecting specimens."

"I stuffed a what? Oh, now I get it." Joshua laughed. "That wasn't a fish. I thought I saw a rare coin in the water, and I scooped it up and hid it in my shirt. I didn't think anyone saw me."

"You're interested in rare coins?" Henry said. "So that was you snooping around our cabin that night!"

Joshua looked embarrassed. "I'm afraid it was. To tell the truth, we're treasure hunters, not sailors.

"From the way he talked, I thought Benny had found a doubloon. I didn't realize it was worthless." He paused. "The only valuable thing I found here was the conch shell and it was cracked."

"You took my conch shell?" Violet asked.

Joshua looked embarrassed, realizing his slip. "I wanted to show it to one of my investors. I wasn't sure how rare it really was."

"What did you do with it?" Melanie asked.

"I stuffed it in a drawer in the classroom," Joshua said defiantly. "I figured you'd find it eventually."

Everyone was silent for a moment, and then Jessie spoke up. "We even suspected you, Nick. Someone took a powerboat out one night, and we found a key ring with the initials NS lying on the seat."

"I can explain that," Nick said. "NS stands for North Star. They're a big coral wholesaler. Those are probably the people that Katherine was dealing with."

Violet reached down to pet the tabby cat who was rubbing against her legs. "At least we know now that Horace didn't scratch Katherine." She saw the surprised look on Nick's face. "Her legs were all scratched from the mangrove trees on Melanie's island, and she blamed it on poor Horace."

"Breaking into someone's cabin is against camp rules," Melanie said sternly to Joshua Slade. "You won't be welcome here again."

"I'm sorry about that," Joshua said softly. He looked at his wife and they turned and walked back to their cabin.

"All those times they acted friendly," Violet remarked, "they were just trying to see if we knew about any sunken treasure."

Benny stifled a yawn. "I can't believe the mystery is all solved," he said sleepily.

"And just in time," Violet said. She glanced at her watch. "Grandfather will be here in just a few hours to pick us up."

"You did a great job, kids," Nick said.

He stepped through the crowd to shake hands with each of them. "Without you, Katherine could have moved on to other sites and other coral beds. It might have taken months, or even years, to catch up with her."

"I'm glad we could help," Henry said. He looked at Benny, who was leaning against him with his eyes half closed. "But now I think it's time to say good night. My little brother is sleeping standing up."

"I'm awake," Benny protested drowsily. As soon as Henry lifted him up, Benny's eyes shut and he snuggled against his older brother.

"Good night," Melanie said softly. "I'll see you in the morning before you leave. Let's have breakfast together."

Grandfather arrived bright and early the following morning. "I'm so glad to see you!" he said, hugging Violet, Jessie, Henry, and Soo Lee. They were already packed and waiting by the camp entrance.

"We spent days out on the water," Jessie said. "It was wonderful."

"But where's Benny?" Grandfather asked, looking around.

"He's here," Violet said playfully. "He's down by the shore. He has something special he wants to show you." She took Grandfather's hand. "Come on, I'll take you there."

"Whatever you say," Grandfather said good-naturedly. He was so happy to see his grandchildren. He missed them, even if they were only away for a few days.

"Tell us about your trip, Grandfather," Henry said.

"It was very relaxing," Grandfather began. "I did a little sailing and I — " He broke off suddenly as they approached the beach. "Is that Benny?"

"It sure is!" Jessie said proudly.

All the children watched as a small figure skimmed over the water on a bright red wind-surfer.

Henry whistled under his breath. "He really got the hang of it," he said admiringly.

"He wanted you to be proud of him, Grandfather."

"Well, I am," Mr. Alden replied, waving to Benny as he zigzagged toward the shore. "I'm proud of all my grandchildren." He moved forward to greet Benny as he neared the shore. "And what have the rest of you been doing while Benny learned wind-surfing? Did anything special happen?"

Violet and Jessie exchanged a look and burst out laughing. "Anything special! Grandfather, we solved another mystery!"

"Tell me about it," he said as Benny ran along the sand toward him.

"It will take a long time," Soo Lee pointed out. "It's a long story."

Grandfather gave Benny a bear hug and scooped him up in his arms. "That's all right," he said, heading back to the car. "We have a long drive back to the Miami airport. But nothing will make the time go faster than hearing about your adventures!"

THE SUMMER CAMP MYSTERY

created by
GERTRUDE CHANDLER WARNER

Illustrated by Hodges Soileau

ALBERT WHITMAN & Company
Morton Grove, Illinois

The Summer Camp Mystery
created by Gertrude Chandler Warner;
illustrated by Hodges Soileau.

ISBN 10: 0-8075-5479-0
ISBN 13: 978-0-8075-5479-1

For more information about Albert Whitman & Company,
visit our web site at www.albertwhitman.com.

Contents

CHAPTER 1

Shapes in the Fog

At five o'clock on an August morning, the sun hadn't risen yet, but the Alden family was already up and about. The streetlamps were still on. In a few minutes, the headlights on James Alden's car were on, too.

Four sleepy children trooped down the porch steps of the big white house where they lived. They joined their grandfather, who was already in the car.

"Buckle up, everyone," Grandfather Alden said. "We want to get an early start driving to Maine."

One by one, Henry, Jessie, Violet, and six-year-old Benny Alden slipped into Grandfather's car. They buckled themselves in.

Mr. Alden backed out slowly. He didn't want to scrape the bottom of his car. It was riding low, loaded down with camp trunks, backpacks, and the five Aldens.

The family housekeeper, Mrs. McGregor, stood by the driveway holding on to Watch, the family dog. "Good-bye, children," Mrs. McGregor said. "Have fun at Camp Sea-gull. Don't eat too much lobster!"

Twelve-year-old Jessie tried not to yawn. She'd barely had time to braid her long brown hair and find her Junior Counselor cap. "Good-bye, Mrs. McGregor. Take good care of Watch for me."

" 'Bye, Mrs. McGregor," the other three children said.

Watch looked at the car with his saddest face. He whined softly, the way he always did when he was left behind.

"Watch wants to come to Camp Seagull with us, too," Jessie said with a little catch in her voice. "I'm going to miss having him sleep at the foot of my bed."

Benny took one last look at Watch and Mrs. McGregor before Mr. Alden pulled away. "Too bad Watch can't be a camper, too. Remember how he found us in our boxcar in the woods — even before you found us, Grandfather?"

Mr. Alden smiled. Benny was quite a chatterbox, even at five o'clock in the morning. "You won't need Watch for company, Benny. The camp is filled with children your age."

"Jessie and I will be right there as Junior Counselors," fourteen-year-old Henry told Benny. "Violet is a camper, too."

"Don't forget," Grandfather Alden said to Benny, "at the end of each day at camp, you'll be joining me at the Dark Harbor Inn."

Violet, who was ten, thought about this. "But the rest of us will be away for the whole week since we're overnight campers.

I'm going to miss you, Grandfather."

"And I'll miss you," Mr. Alden said in a quiet voice. "While I catch up on my reading, you can catch up on your painting and your crafts."

Violet's eyes brightened. "I'm going to spend as much time as I can in the art studio at camp."

Jessie was bubbling with plans. "I'm so glad Ginny and Rich Gullen found room for us in this session of Camp Seagull, Grandfather. There's so much going on. Last night, I looked over the counselor manual again. There's waterskiing, Costume Night, swimming, storytelling, arts and crafts, sports — you name it."

"Eating. You forgot to say eating," Benny said.

Everyone in the car laughed. Who else in the Alden family would be thinking about food so early in the morning?

"Don't worry, Benny, you won't go hungry," Henry said.

"I know. I never go hungry. See?" Benny pulled a bag from the backpack at his feet.

"Mrs. McGregor said it was a long way to Maine. I wanted to be ready, so I packed some trail mix."

"But Benny, we're not going on any trails today," Henry pointed out. "Not until we get out to Claw Island, where Camp Seagull is. You don't need trail mix riding in a car."

Benny disagreed. "Trail mix is good anytime, even on long car rides." He took out some sunflower seeds to munch on. "Especially on long car rides."

Just as the sun came up, Mr. Alden turned onto the busy highway going north. "Off we go, children!"

"Good-bye, Greenfield," Violet said. "See you next week."

By the time Mr. Alden drove into northern Maine, the gas tank was nearly empty. As for the picnic basket Mrs. McGregor had sent along, that was nearly empty, too. And so was Benny's trail mix bag.

Mr. Alden shifted in his seat. He'd been driving a long time. "We're practically there, children. Now that we're off the main highway, let's look for road signs. There's some fog rolling in. I don't want to miss the turnoff for the Claw Island ferry. It's just outside Dark Harbor. I went there all the time when I was a boy."

"Now Henry and I are the boys!" Benny said proudly. "And we're visiting Claw Island just like you did."

"Right you are." Grandfather smiled to himself. "Only there wasn't a camp on the island back then, just the old Pines estate that the family owned, along with some deserted buildings. Many a time my chums and I would go out to Claw Island to explore and play games."

"Just like us — if we ever get there." Benny pressed his forehead against the window.

Violet stared out, too. "The fog has swallowed up everything except for the pointy pine trees."

"Look! There's a sign!" Benny made a claw with his hand. "Why is it called Claw Island, anyway?"

"If you look at a map, you can see the island is shaped like a lobster claw," Jessie explained.

Mr. Alden turned onto a sandy beach road. "And so it was in my grandmother's day. Only back then it was called Claw Point, not Claw Island. It was still connected to the mainland just outside Dark Harbor. One summer, Grandmother returned to discover the ocean had washed away the road. Two hurricanes later, the ocean covered over the beach and the dunes in between."

Jessie flipped through the Camp Seagull manual. "It says here that after the second hurricane, the Pines family turned their property into a camp. Then last winter they sold it to Rich and Ginny Gullen, the new owners."

Mr. Alden drove slowly down the dirt road. "I hope the Gullens make a go of it. Rich told me the Pines family found it difficult running a camp on the island. They had to sell it because they lost too much money. As you can see, it's not an easy place to get to. It can only be reached by boat. People travel out on the small passenger ferry. Camp supplies go on the freight boat once a week."

"We're on the people boat," Benny said. "I just hope the food boat doesn't get lost."

Grandfather smiled. "That's not likely to happen. It's only a ten-minute boat ride from here. Too bad it's foggy right now. On a sunny day, Claw Island is a very pretty sight."

"But not today," Violet said. "There's no sign of the island, just dark shapes and fog everywhere."

Grandfather Alden brought the car to a stop in a small parking area. "Here's the ferry landing, just where it used to be. I see a few other camp families have already arrived."

The Aldens scrambled from the car. They needed to stretch their legs after their long trip. They followed the sound of the lapping ocean right down to a small beach and an empty dock.

The children looked out at the gray water. A few seagulls bobbed in the cove, ducking under now and then for a fish. Everything else was wrapped in fog and strangely silent.

The Aldens returned to the parking area. They looked shyly at the other families milling around in the mist. Some of the children already had on their Camp Seagull shirts. Most of the younger children stayed close to their families, just as Benny and Violet stayed next to Grandfather Alden. Everyone would be saying good-bye soon enough.

CHAPTER 2

Screams on the Beach

Henry and Jessie helped unload Grandfather's car. They carried their trunks toward the dock, where other campers were lining up their luggage.

Jessie smiled at a sandy-haired girl with a ponytail and a Junior Counselor cap. "Hi," she said.

The girl kept on counting the bags and trunks. She didn't seem to hear Jessie.

Jessie greeted the girl again. "I'm Jessie Alden. That's my brother Henry over there. He's also a Junior Counselor. We can help you carry the baggage onto the dock if you'd like."

The girl picked up a heavy duffel bag. "You have to have special counselor training first before you can do certain things. Leave your camp trunks on the beach. I'll put them on the ferry." With that, the girl turned back to her work.

Jessie returned to the other Aldens. "I must have said the wrong thing to that Junior Counselor. I'll wait to ask her what to do when she's not so busy."

Raaaangh!

Several children screamed. Even the grown-ups jumped at the earsplitting sound. Everyone looked around. There was nothing to be seen through the fog.

"Ha! You lose points already," someone nearby said, then cackled. "No screaming at the horn."

Benny stood by Jessie. "Who said that? What are they talking about? It's so foggy, I can't tell what's going on."

Jessie gave Benny a friendly squeeze. "I think they're talking about the No Screaming Medal. It's part of the Camp Seagull Olympics. Campers try to win points for being brave, or neat, or helpful—or quiet."

Henry explained, "The No Screaming Medal goes to the group that has the fewest screamers. There are all kinds of other awards, too. There's a No Food on the Floor Award for the group that drops the least food in the dining hall."

"They give awards for things like that?" Benny asked. "That's easy. I just hope they don't have a No Talking Medal."

Raaaangh! The horn sounded again, even louder.

Everyone jumped. But no one screamed this time.

Where was that terrible sound coming from? The Aldens stared out at the water. A boat, more like a large raft with a railing and a bench all around, chugged toward the shore. At the wheel, an unsmiling man in a pilot's cap looked over the side of the boat to line it up with the dock.

Onboard sat two children, both with curly dark hair. The boy looked about

Jessie's age. The girl seemed to be a few years younger, about nine years old. Both children stared back at the campers on the beach without smiling.

One of the nearby campers whispered to the Aldens, "The boatman is named Booth Pines. But all the campers call him Boo. He shows up in different places to fix things, and you don't know he's there."

The Aldens looked at one another. Camp Seagull seemed a little spookier than they had expected from the camp photographs they had seen.

Benny tapped Grandfather's arm. "Is that the people ferry?"

Mr. Alden smiled. "You can call it that. It's such a short distance to Claw Island, you could almost float over there on a log."

Everyone jumped back when Mr. Pines threw out a heavy rope. Henry grabbed the rope to tie it to the dock.

"Leave that!" the man yelled.

Henry dropped the rope. "Sorry. Just trying to help."

Mr. Pines turned off the ferry engine

then stepped down. "You can help by standing back. Can't have a bunch of strange kids bringing in the boat. There could be some big problems if the ferry floated away."

"Oh, I know lots of sailor knots," Henry explained. "But I don't want to get in your way."

Mr. Pines turned to the boy on the ferry. "Zach, go tie that rope good and tight."

The boy stepped down on the dock. "Sure thing, Dad." The boy, tall like his father, wound the rope around the dock piling.

"Now go help Kim bring up the luggage," the man told his son before turning to the girl. "Lizzie, stay onboard. Zach and Kim will bring up the trunks and duffel bags. Push them under the seats so the weight's even all around."

Zach joined the Junior Counselor who had been collecting the campers' trunks. Together, they began to load the luggage onto the ferry.

The Aldens wanted to help, but they held back. They didn't want the man to scold them the way he had yelled at Henry.

Mr. Alden stepped forward. He studied the man's face before speaking. "Glad to meet you, sir. I'm James Alden. My grandchildren will be staying at Camp Seagull. We'd be glad to lend a hand."

The boatman stared at Mr. Alden for a few seconds. "My children, Zach and Lizzie, are stronger than they look. They know more than anyone here about what needs to be done."

The Aldens stepped away. They found a nearby dune to sit on while they waited for the ferry to be ready.

A few minutes later, a van pulled up. The door opened. A short-haired woman with a big smile stepped out of the van, holding a clipboard. "Mr. Alden!" the woman said. She put out her hand. "Ginny Gullen. Remember me? Of course, I was Ginny Shore way back when I worked at the Dark Harbor Inn. You visited every summer. I remember how you enjoyed having your morning coffee on the porch."

Mr. Alden broke into a big smile. "Virginia Shore! My, my, you're all grown up now. It took a few minutes to connect the face with the name. I've spoken on the phone with your husband, Rich, to make the arrangements for my grandchildren. They're so happy you were able to find spots for them in camp at the last minute."

The Aldens noticed that Mr. Pines and his children frowned when Grandfather said this.

Ginny turned to the Alden children. "Let me guess. Henry, Jessie, Violet. And you're Benny, right?"

"Right," Benny said proudly.

Ginny waved over Zach Pines. He put down the duffel bags he was carrying. "Come meet the Aldens, Zach," Ginny said. "Here are Henry, Jessie, Violet, and Benny. Everybody, meet Zach Pines. His father, Booth, is our ferry pilot and our all-around groundskeeper and assistant. Zach's sister, Lizzie, is also a camper. They live in Dark Harbor now, but they practically grew up on Claw Island. These two know Camp Seagull inside and out."

The Aldens crowded around Zach Pines like a flock of birds. When they noticed Zach seemed shy because of all the attention, they stepped back a little.

Ginny smoothed things over in her cheery way. "Thanks to you, Henry, Zach won't have to run the Flag Ceremony twice a day. He's been doing that since before Rich and I took over," Ginny informed the Aldens. "Now he doesn't have to rush in the morning and after dinner."

"Ginny asked me to pack my bugle," Henry proudly told Zach. "I learned to play it for flag raising in the Scouts."

Zach didn't say anything. He looked as if he wanted to escape the five pairs of eyes fixed on him. "My father needs me now," Zach said before sprinting off to the dock.

"I don't know what Rich and I would do without the Pines family," Ginny said. "I do want Zach and Lizzie to enjoy camp as much as the other campers. Booth is a good father, but he's very serious. He sometimes forgets to let the children relax and have fun." She turned to Henry and Jessie. "I've assigned some of Zach and Lizzie's responsibilities to both of you. I'd like them to have some more free time to take part in camp activities."

"Are they overnight campers?" Jessie asked.

Ginny frowned. "I'm afraid not. Rich and I didn't have any more cabin spaces for overnight campers. Zach and Lizzie are day campers. Still, I want them to have a great time, just like everyone else. I'm dividing up some of the chores Booth has given them and assigning them to Junior Counselors like yourselves. In fact, you can go help them load the ferry right now."

Henry and Jessie stared at each other.

"Ummm . . . we tried to help," Henry said, "but Mr. Pines said he didn't want any new kids slowing things up."

"The other Junior Counselor who's helping out said we have to have special training first," Jessie added.

Ginny's smile froze for a second. "Oh, dear. Let me speak to Booth. He's used to doing things his way. I suppose he didn't want any new campers underfoot yet. But your grandfather told my husband what careful, hard workers you are. As for Kim Waters, I sent her over from camp to greet the new campers. I better straighten things out now that I'm here."

The Aldens overheard Ginny talking to Mr. Pines. "Booth, I have two strong helpers here — Henry and Jessie Alden," she said to the boatman.

Kim came over to Ginny. "Hi, Ginny. We still have some more trunks and duffels to get on the ferry."

Ginny had a different idea. "Kim, loading bags isn't what I had in mind for you. I sent you over to welcome the new campers and make them feel at home. I'd like the Aldens to meet you. This is Kim Waters. Kim, meet Mr. Alden and his grandchildren Henry, Jessie, Violet, and Benny. Henry and Jessie are Junior Counselors like you. Violet's one of our overnight campers. And Benny is a day camper."

The girl nodded but didn't say anything even after the Aldens said hello. Instead she turned to Ginny. "I have to finish helping Boo — I mean, Mr. Pines. I know where everything goes," the girl said. "The new campers are still with their families."

"Please attend to the campers," Ginny reminded Kim.

Finally, Kim took a whistle from her pocket and blew it. "Campers, over here! The ferry's about to leave. Let's move it!"

Ginny sighed. "Gentle with the new campers, Kim. They're nervous about leaving their families. You know what? Finish loading the luggage after all. The Aldens can help board the campers."

"Fine with me. That's what I wanted to do anyway," Kim said before heading to the ferry.

Henry and Jessie rounded up the campers. They led them to the boat, talking to them gently so they would look forward to their ferry trip to camp.

"Greetings, Seagulls!" Ginny began, smiling at the children gathered near the dock. "Welcome to Camp Seagull. I'm Ginny Gullen. I'm so glad to meet you at last. We have three Junior Counselors here: Henry and Jessie Alden — and that's Kim Waters over there. Kim is a fifth-year Seagull camper. Now she's a Junior Counselor, too. She'll make sure your luggage gets on board safe and sound."

Henry and Jessie stood aside as the new and old campers said good-bye to their families.

Ginny checked off the children's names. "Mr. Pines is our ferry pilot. He'll bring us out to the island. When we arrive, we'll all gather by the flagpole in front of Evergreen Lodge. Parents and grandparents, please meet your day campers at seven-thirty tonight right here. That's when the ferry brings them back after Flag Ceremony. Now it's time for good-bye hugs, everyone!"

Mr. Alden put his hand on Benny's shoulder. "I'll be right by the dock when the ferry comes in this evening, Benny."

Grandfather turned to Violet. "Enjoy your stay. If you think of your lonesome grandfather when you're in arts and crafts,

I could use another leather change purse or a new coffee mug."

Violet hugged Grandfather. "I'll make you something special."

"And keep an eye on Henry and Jessie," Grandfather told Violet and Benny. "Make sure they have fun. Being Junior Counselors isn't all work."

"You know us, Grandfather," Henry said. "Work is fun for us."

The four Aldens were the last campers to board. " 'Bye, Grandfather," they called out.

Raaaangh! the horn screamed. The ferry pulled away from the dock.

Everyone turned to wave to the families onshore.

That's when Jessie spotted something on the beach that wasn't supposed to be there. She turned to Henry. "Look!" she whispered. "Our trunks are still on the beach — off to the side. See? Kim told me she'd take care of them."

Henry smacked his forehead. "Oh, no!"

Jessie rolled her eyes. "Let's not bother Ginny right now," she whispered. "She's busy. After all, we're Junior Counselors. We're supposed to know better."

"When we get to camp, I'll ask Ginny if Mr. Pines can safely store our trunks tonight when he drops off the day campers," Jessie said. "Maybe he can bring them out in the morning."

This was too much for Kim Waters, who overheard Jessie. "This is the first day of camp," she said. "The Gullens and Boo have a lot of jobs at the camp. They don't have time to make special trips to Dark Harbor all because people leave their things behind."

"But when I wanted to help with the trunks, you told me . . ." Jessie stopped. "Never mind. We'll be more careful next time."

When the Aldens looked back at the beach, the fog had swallowed it up along with their three camp trunks.

CHAPTER 3

Monster Rock

Just as Booth Pines guided the passenger ferry across the water, the fog lifted. Grandfather Alden had been right. Up ahead, a very pretty sight appeared: Claw Island sparkled in the water.

From the boat, the Aldens could see cozy wooden buildings tucked into groves of tall pine trees. A flagpole rose above the large main building.

Jessie grabbed Henry's arm. "The island is so close. I wonder if we could swim between Dark Harbor and Claw Island. After all, we just passed our lifesaving test at the Greenfield Pool."

"You're not allowed," Zach Pines told Jessie. "There are strong currents between the island and Dark Harbor. You could get sucked out to sea."

When some of the younger children heard this, they moved closer to Henry and Jessie.

"Oh, I was just wondering, that's all," Jessie said. She turned to some of the younger children. "My counselor manual said the swimming lessons are given on the bay side of the island. The water is warm and calm there—like a lake."

"Look, a whale!" Benny cried. He pointed to something wide, smooth, and gray off in the water not too far from Claw Island.

The campers swiveled around to see the whale.

"That's Monster Rock, not a whale," Lizzie Pines informed Benny. "When it gets dark, the rock can turn into a monster that comes out of the water. Sometimes we even find giant footprints in the sand."

"Goodness, this isn't the time for that old made-up tale, Lizzie!" Ginny said when she noticed the worried looks of some of the new campers. "Actually, children, that's Seal Rock. Often, if the sun is out and the tide is low, seals climb onto the rock to sun themselves."

With the fog and Monster Rock behind them and Camp Seagull in front of them, the campers had a hard time sitting still. Camp was about to begin!

Onshore, a circle of campers who had arrived earlier stood around the flagpole. Behind them a group of teenagers and young adults waved their Senior and Junior Counselor caps at everyone on the ferry.

"Welcome, Seagulls!" the flagpole crowd yelled out. "Give us a seagull squawk!"

The new campers weren't sure what to do.

"Go ahead," Ginny urged everyone.

"Crawk! Crawk!" the campers screamed out like a flock of seagulls about to land on Claw Island.

"The camp is so pretty," Violet said when

she stepped onto the dock. "Evergreen Lodge looks just the way I pictured — with porches and big windows looking out on the bay."

"You know," Benny said, "Claw Island doesn't look a bit like a scary lobster claw."

"That's only on a map, Benny," Violet said, laughing. "Or if you're a bird looking down."

Ginny waved the campers toward the flag-pole group. "There's my husband, Rich."

Rich and Ginny Gullen wore identical CAMP SEAGULL DIRECTOR shirts and nearly identical friendly smiles.

"Greetings," Rich began. "Welcome to Camp Seagull. Hope you had a smooth ride over. Ginny and I are happy to welcome you to our first season as directors of Camp Seagull. The camp has been around since Ginny and I grew up in Dark Harbor. Both of us worked here when we weren't much older than most of you."

Ginny looked around at the campers. "I know some of your parents were once campers here. We've kept up many of the traditions the Pines family started in the past. And we've added a few of our own."

The Aldens noticed Mr. Pines and his children didn't seem in a hurry to join the group.

"Is Mr. Pines related to the family that owned the camp?" Jessie asked Kim in a whisper.

"Yes," Kim whispered back. "But he doesn't mention it. His family had to give up the camp. Now he has to work for Rich and Ginny. They changed everything from before."

"Do you still have Dress Your Favorite Fruit Night?" a girl camper asked Rich.

Rich grinned. "At Camp Seagull we even dress up vegetables! Our campers last session voted to have a Dress Your Favorite Vegetable Night. We've added new activities like that. But it's still the same special place it's always been. Now Ginny will tell you all about the Camp Seagull Olympics."

"Okay, campers. Let's start by lining up," Ginny began. She picked up a big blue bowl. "Come and choose a surprise from this bowl."

Benny tried to peek over the rim of the bowl. "Is it a snack?"

Ginny held the bowl out for Benny. "You'll see."

Benny reached in. "It's a little dolphin." He showed Violet the small plastic animal.

"I picked a seal," she said.

"I got a dolphin," Jessie said after her turn. "So did Henry."

When the bowl was empty, Ginny looked around at all the campers. "During your stay, you'll either be on a dolphin or a seal team, depending on the animal you chose. Half our cabins are Dolphin cabins, and half are Seal cabins. Even day campers have a cabin to spend time in during the day. As for you overnight campers, after our first Flag Ceremony, Mr. Pines will move your trunks and duffels to your cabins."

"Except yours," Zach muttered before stepping away from Henry.

Ginny waited for the campers to settle

down. "Here's how our Olympics work. Dolphins and Seals try to get points for our activities and events, as well as for doing good things around camp."

"Like making our beds, right?" a girl around Benny's age asked. "My brother told me. And not screaming at the ferry horn. Only I did 'cause I forgot."

"And shooting a gazillion baskets in basketball," another boy added. "When my dad was a camper, his team won the Olympics. He was a good basketball player a long time ago."

"Up until this year, my groups won every single year," Kim announced. "I've been playing soccer and basketball since I was little. I won lots of points in the Camp Seagull Olympics. But not this year."

"How come?" one of the new campers wanted to know.

"I was a Junior Counselor for the Dolphins last session," Kim answered bitterly. "But we lost. Sports don't count as much anymore. The Olympics are *way* harder to win now."

"No fair," said the boy with the basketball player dad.

Ginny waited for the campers to quiet down. "Well, Rich and I did make a few changes in the Olympics. We wanted to make it easier for all campers to earn points, even those who aren't sports stars. So now campers think up new activities together that everyone can be good at — even if you don't play a sport."

"Like not talking too much, right?" Benny asked. "That's what my brother, Henry, told me. Only I talk a lot, so the Dolphins might not win for that."

Ginny tried not to laugh, but she couldn't help it. "Well, Benny, maybe you'll win the Make Somebody Laugh Award. Last session, the Seals thought up that activity."

Ginny held up a blue notebook. "In here, you'll find a list of fun Olympic activities from last session. You'll also get to add new ones when you go to your cabins later. Your counselor will make a list of all your ideas. Then each cabin will choose the one idea that best pulls the whole camp together and give it to me or Rich for our Big Idea Medal."

Rich continued where Ginny left off. "This medal is worth a hundred points to the winning side. Now we will officially begin camp with our first Camp Seagull Flag Ceremony."

The next thing the campers heard was a scratchy sound that filled the air. The campers covered their ears as the loud notes of a bugle blared out from a tape recorder.

"Hear ye! Hear ye, campers!" Rich called out over the loudspeaker. "Sorry we don't have a live bugler yet. We will when Henry Alden's bugle arrives with his trunk. What you just heard is the famous Camp Seagull bugle recording. Our new Junior Counselor Henry Alden will conduct the Flag Ceremony this session."

Henry stepped forward with the American flag and the Camp Seagull flag. As he had learned to do in the Scouts, Henry carefully unfolded the flags and fastened them to the ropes. As he guided the flags slowly up the pole, the campers watched in silence.

When both flags reached the top, Rich started the bugle tape again. The whole camp broke into a cheer.

"Let Camp Seagull begin!" Rich cried out over the cheers and the last notes of the crackling bugle tape.

The campers gave the Camp Seagull cheer. *"Crawk! Crawk!"* they all cried.

"Crawk! Crawk!" a seagull answered from its perch on the top of the flagpole.

After the Flag Ceremony, Ginny assigned each counselor to a group of campers.

"Let's find Violet," Henry suggested to Jessie and Benny. "I want to wish her luck before we go to our cabins."

They found Violet sitting cross-legged on the ground a few feet away from Kim Waters. Kim had a clipboard in front of her. She was speaking with her campers one by one.

When she saw her family, Violet scram-

bled to her feet. "My group is getting ready to go to our cabin," Violet said.

"I wish you were on the Dolphin team," Benny said. "Aldens like to stay together."

Violet's eyes darkened. "I know. At least you'll be with Henry. And I'll be near Jessie's cabin. Birch — that's the name of our cabin — is only two cabins away from hers. Maybe we can visit back and forth."

Jessie hugged Violet. "We'll all see one another at activities and meals, though not overnight."

"Violet Alden!" Kim yelled out. "Over here with the Seals. We have to get to Birch Cabin — on the double!"

Violet gave Jessie one last hug. " 'Bye. See you at dinner," she said.

Kim blew her whistle again. "The Seals sit together at meals," she told her campers. "Now what we're going to do is come up with the best Big Idea in the whole camp. This session, the Seals are going to win the Olympics. No matter what."

"Why is Kim so grouchy?" Benny asked. "I'm glad I'm a Dolphin."

"Maybe Kim wanted to be in the Dolphins again," Jessie guessed. "Well, time to go to our cabins with our campers. See you later, Benny. 'Bye, Henry."

CHAPTER 4

Boo!

Henry and Dave Baylor, a Senior Counselor, were in charge of the six- and seven-year-old Dolphin boys. They introduced themselves to the campers. Since Dave had work to do at the waterfront, Henry led the boys to the cabin on his own. "This way, Dolphins. Driftwood Cabin is just down the Interstate."

"Henry's kidding," Benny explained in case the other boys didn't get Henry's joke. "The Interstate doesn't go to Claw Island, just the Boo boat."

Henry noticed Zach pushing a cart piled high with duffel bags and trunks. "Hey, Zach, we're going the same way. That cart looks heavy. Want some help?"

"I don't need any help," Zach answered.

"Sorry about leaving our bags onshore," Henry said. "We didn't mean to make more work for you and your dad. When Dave comes back from the waterfront, maybe I can help you finish unloading the ferry."

"I told you, I don't need any help," Zach said. "I'm still in charge of luggage. You're in charge of the Flag Ceremony now. Let's keep it that way." Zach then pushed the cart so hard, it nearly tipped over on a tree root.

"How come Zach doesn't like you?" Benny whispered.

"I wish I knew," Henry said.

When Henry arrived at Driftwood Cabin with his group, Boo Pines was nailing some loose boards on the screen door.

"Boo!" one of the boys said.

Boo Pines didn't even look up.

"Let's not bother Mr. Pines," Henry told the boys. "First we'll unpack so we can make up our bunks."

"But you don't have a trunk," a boy named Sam said.

"Not yet," Henry said, "but it'll be here tomorrow. My bugle's in it. I'll teach you to play a few notes."

Benny was proud of his older brother. "Henry's the new bugle player and flag-raiser person," he announced.

"What about Zach?" Sam asked. "How come he's not doing it? That was his job last session."

Slam! Slam! All the boys, even Henry, jumped when the screen door banged so hard it shook the cabin.

"Something the matter?" Henry called out.

Out on the cabin porch, Boo shut the lid of his toolbox. The next sounds the boys heard were Boo's heavy work boots thumping down the steps. When Henry looked out, Boo had disappeared into the woods.

* * *

"Welcome to Cedar Cabin, Dolphins," Jessie began when her campers stepped inside. "It looks a little bare right now, but not for long. We'll fix it up so it's nice and cozy. My brothers and sister and I used to live in a boxcar in the woods. We made it like a real house."

"I wish our cabin was a boxcar," one of the campers said. "Will you tell us stories about living in the woods?"

"Lots of them," Jessie said, "including how our dog, Watch, found us. But first I need to get Lizzie Pines here. She's a day camper, but she's supposed to be in Cedar Cabin right now."

Jessie dug into her backpack. "Here's a piece of paper and a pencil, girls. I'll draw a squiggle on it. Then you girls pass it around and see if you can turn the squiggle into a picture by the time I get back with Lizzie. Here comes Sarah, our Senior Counselor. She'll stay with you while I fetch Lizzie. Hi, Sarah."

Outside, Jessie headed toward the ferry

landing. She spotted Lizzie and Zach talking.

"But I don't want to be a Dolphin," Jessie overheard Lizzie telling Zach when she got closer. "I want to be with Kim like last time. She said I could help her win the Olympics like we used to all the time before Ginny and Rich came. Maybe Kim will let me stay overnight in Birch Cabin. Then I can be an overnight camper like Dad promised."

Zach turned to his sister. "Look, Lizzie, you have to go along with the Aldens. Ginny and Rich are in charge now, not Dad. But there are lots of ways you can help Kim."

"Lizzie!" Jessie yelled out without coming closer. She didn't want Zach and Lizzie to know she had heard them talking about her. She motioned Lizzie to return to Cedar Cabin. Jessie walked back alone, wondering what was going on. What did Zach mean about Lizzie helping Kim?

"Squiggles was a good game for the girls," Sarah said when Jessie returned. "I have to run to the office. Be back soon."

A redheaded camper named Laura handed Jessie a sheet of paper. "Here's what we drew."

"A boxcar!" Jessie said, admiring the girls' drawing.

"Where's Lizzie?" Laura asked.

Jessie stuck her head out the door. Lizzie was coming toward the cabin. "She's right behind me. Let's carry in all of your trunks. I'll help you unpack now that Lizzie's on her way."

Lizzie was on her way — but not to Cedar Cabin. Instead, she stopped off at Birch Cabin.

All the Birch campers, except for Violet, had their trunks and duffels open. Violet was helping Kim unpack.

"Clean towels stay folded in the trunks," Kim told Violet. "I guess your sister and brother didn't read the rules. Especially the one saying not to leave your trunks on the beach."

Violet tried not to think about her neatly packed trunk sitting in Dark Harbor. She

looked up when Lizzie came in. "Did Jessie send you over to tell me something?"

"No," Lizzie answered. "I came to see Kim."

Kim turned around. "What's up, Lizzie? I was hoping you'd be in my group. I have to teach my campers everything, even not to forget their trunks."

"I have a message," Lizzie said. She handed Kim a piece of paper.

Kim read it over. "Hmmm. I guess it's okay. You'd better go to your own cabin now."

Lizzie didn't move. "Can't I stay a little longer? Or overnight? I'm sure my dad would let me. I could put a sleeping bag in the corner. I wouldn't take up much room."

Violet had an idea, but she was too shy to say anything right away. Finally she decided to speak up. "What if Lizzie and I switch? That way she could be a Seal and stay here in Birch since you're friends already."

Kim and Lizzie looked at each other.

"Please, Kim," Lizzie pleaded. "Can I stay here?"

Before Kim had time to answer, there was a knock on the cabin door.

"Come in," Kim called out. "Oh, hi, Sarah. I thought the Senior Counselors had a meeting in the office."

"It's over," Sarah said. She looked around until she spotted Lizzie sitting on Kim's bed. "Aha! I see you kidnapped one of my favorite campers," Sarah joked. "Lizzie, I think you forgot which cabin you were assigned to. You're with Jessie Alden and me over in Cedar. It's time to start the fun. We can't do that if one of the Dolphins in our pod is missing. Let's go, kiddo. Jessie's waiting."

Lizzie didn't move from Kim's bed. "But . . . but, we were just talking about Violet changing places and being a Dolphin instead. Then I could stay in Kim's group like last session."

"No way!" Sarah said, smiling. "Last session, you were such a great camper, I kept wishing you were on my team. And now you are. Off we go!"

Violet looked on as Sarah led Lizzie back to Cedar Cabin. She tried not to think about how strange everything seemed on her first night at camp. Jessie was just two cabins away, but that seemed as far away as Greenfield.

"I have an extra stuffed animal," one of the girls said, holding out a floppy fur rabbit. "You can borrow him until your trunk comes, Violet."

"If it comes," Kim said before shutting the lid of her own trunk.

CHAPTER 5

Footprints in the Sand

A spiral of blue-gray smoke arose from the campfire near Evergreen Lodge. The hamburger and hot dog smells from Camp Seagull's first cookout began to fade. Now that the day was nearly over, the first day of camp was fading, too.

Benny pulled his stick from the fire. On the end was a melted, golden brown marshmallow. He slid it between two graham crackers and a piece of chocolate. "Yum," he said after tasting his s'more treat. "Cookouts are my favorite."

"So are breakfast, lunch, and dinner," Henry kidded.

Jessie and Violet laughed at Henry's joke, along with the campers nearby.

"I'm glad Kim let us sit together for dessert," Violet told Jessie.

"Me, too," Jessie said. "Here, you can have my s'more. I'm full from our cookout," Jessie said. "Are you having fun with the Seals?"

Violet stared into the fire. "I'll like camp better when I can go on nature walks or start making pottery. Kim is upset with our cabin because of my trunk. She said I lost points for our team."

Jessie frowned. "Well, be sure to mention that since Henry and I are both Dolphins, our team will lose twice as many points for leaving our trunks behind. Ginny was a little upset, but she asked Mr. Pines to bring them to camp tomorrow morning when he drops off the day campers."

Violet wriggled her toes to warm them near the fire. "I'll still lose for cabin inspection. Kim's cross with me."

"That's just her way," Jessie said. "She's probably upset that Rich and Ginny changed the Olympics from sports to a lot of other activities. Don't worry. You'll help the Seals win with your crafts and the way you help other campers. Oh, listen," Jessie said, "it's the bugle tape again."

"I have a few announcements before Henry takes down the flags for the night," Rich began. "Counselors, remember to walk your campers to the dock at seven-twenty. Mr. Pines will have the ferry ready to bring the day campers back to Dark Harbor for the night."

Benny was glad to hear this. "I like camp," he said to Jessie, "but I like seeing Grandfather 's'more.' "

"Good one," Jessie said, laughing at Benny's joke. "Uh-oh. S'more bugle music is coming on. Let's stand up for Flag Ceremony."

Henry walked over to the flagpole and lowered the camp flags as the campers watched quietly. When the flags reached the bottom of the ropes, everyone cheered for

Henry. He carefully folded the flags for the next day and brought them to Evergreen Lodge.

Jessie's and Henry's Dolphins gathered near one another to walk back to their cabins. The sun slid behind the mountains. The wind picked up and whistled through the pine trees.

"Have you seen Lizzie?" Jessie asked Sarah, the Senior Counselor. "She keeps disappearing on me."

"I saw her with Kim walking to the Bogs — you know, the camp bathrooms," Sarah said. "Go ahead with the other girls. I'll make sure Lizzie gets to the cabin."

"Brrr. I'm an ice cube," Benny said as all the Dolphins made their way through the woods.

"How are we going to stay warm in the cabins when it's so dark and cold?" a girl named Daisy asked Jessie.

"At lights-out, we'll close the shutters and the doors and get under the covers," Jessie said. "The cabins are small. Our body heat will warm them right up."

"Not my body heat," Benny said. "I'm going to be at Grandfather's hotel in a big old bed with lots of quilts."

"Sssh," Henry said. He didn't want his overnight campers to start thinking about the warm beds they left behind at home. "Our cabin will be snug and warm."

"And dark," one little boy said as the groups walked deeper into the woods. "The lights from Evergreen Lodge are getting far away."

"But the light from my flashlight is right here," Henry told his group. He turned on the big flashlight Mrs. McGregor had given him to keep in his backpack. "See?"

The flashlight helped the children find their way through the woods. Unfortunately, the light made the children see shadows everywhere, too.

Daisy stayed close to Jessie. "I wish you'd brought your dog, Watch," she said as everyone huddled near one another on the walk to the cabins. "Look. Now Seal Rock looks like Monster Rock again."

Jessie and Henry looked out over the water. They didn't say anything right away. Indeed, now that evening was coming on, the dark, smooth rock did look like the back of some giant creature in the water.

"It's only the mist and the ocean moving," Jessie said in her soothing voice, "not Monster — I mean, Seal Rock."

The Dolphins weren't far from their cabins when they heard a branch crack in the woods.

"Ooooh! What was that?" Benny said. "Did a tree fall down?"

Jessie stepped ahead. "Watch my campers, Henry. I'll run ahead."

Jessie found her own flashlight. She walked quickly for about ten feet. She noticed a broken tree branch close to Cedar Cabin. She dragged it off the path and walked back to her campers. Jessie shined her flashlight on the damp sandy path. Daisy, still nervous, was right by her side.

"Look!" Daisy screamed.

The other campers screamed, too. They grabbed on to Jessie's arms and legs.

"There, there, girls. Why are you screaming?" she asked her jittery campers.

Daisy pointed to the ground in front of them. "Footprints! Monster footprints!"

Jessie looked closely at the ground. She wanted to believe Daisy's eyes were playing tricks. Then she saw what Daisy saw — huge claw prints, nearly a foot wide, one in front of the other.

Jessie's mind raced. She needed to stay calm for her Dolphins. She waved her flashlight around the nearby woods. She saw two pairs of eyes flash back. But they weren't monster eyes, unless the monsters were wearing Camp Seagull T-shirts. The figures ran off into the woods.

"Somebody played a silly trick on us so we'd scream," Jessie said. "Sarah says one team does that at the end of the week to make the other team lose points. But it's not supposed to happen the first few nights. Our monster didn't come from the ocean but from Camp Seagull.

"And we won't scream again," she went on. "We just have to find the monsters who played the trick."

When the girls arrived at their cabin, Sarah was waiting. "I didn't find Lizzie. I thought she caught up with you. So it *was* you guys screaming outside. That's what Kim said, anyway. She just raced in here to remind me to take away points for screaming."

"Was she wearing a camp T-shirt?" Jessie asked.

"We're all wearing camp T-shirts," Sarah answered with a laugh.

"I wish we weren't going to lose points for screaming," Jessie said. Then she cheered up. "I just thought of something."

A couple of girls pulled on Jessie's sleeves. "What? What?" they asked.

"If we find the person who made the monster footprints, that person's team will lose points for scaring people," Jessie said. "Not that we're scared — right, Dolphins?"

"Right!" the Dolphin girls cheered.

CHAPTER 6

Trouble for Jessie

Jessie's cabin soon sounded as if it were filled with chipmunks. The Cedar Cabin campers were settling in.

"There you are," Jessie said when Lizzie finally showed up for the cabin meeting. "We had a bit of excitement in the woods. Somebody tried to scare us, but we didn't get scared — not too much, anyway. Right, girls?" Jessie asked. "Come on in, Lizzie," Jessie continued. "Leave your sneakers outside, though. They're all wet and sandy.

And next time, stay with our cabin group, okay?"

Lizzie stepped on the porch to remove her sneakers. When she came back, she stood in the doorway barefoot. The other girls arranged themselves on the beds and the floor close to Jessie. Lizzie stayed where she was.

"Okay, Dolphins, let's talk about some ideas you might have for the Big Idea Medal," Jessie began. "I'll write down your ideas. After that, we'll vote on one to give Ginny and Rich."

"I know," Daisy began. "We could have Be Nice Days. We would put slips of paper with our names on them in a box and choose one every day. Then we all would do nice things for that person on her day."

"Or at lights-out time, I could sing my favorite song," another girl piped up. "That's to help anyone who can't fall asleep. My mom does that. Is that good, Jessie?"

"It sure is. I'll write it down on my list."

Jessie found a notepad and began writing the girls' suggestions.

"Can we write down sharing chocolate?" a girl in pigtails asked.

The girls giggled, even Jessie.

Lizzie Pines didn't giggle, though. "Food is not allowed in the cabins," she told everyone. "Junior Counselors have to know the rules."

"Lizzie's right," Jessie said. "No chocolate or any food in Cedar Cabin. Thank you, Lizzie."

"Where's your trunk?" Daisy asked when she noticed Jessie only had a backpack on her bed. "Didn't you bring one?"

Jessie felt her whole face get red, even her ears.

Before Jessie could explain what happened, Lizzie interrupted. "The Aldens left their stuff at the ferry. Cedar Cabin is going to lose points."

"What about your pj's and teddy bear?" Daisy asked Jessie. She double-checked that her own pajamas and teddy bear were right there.

"I'm really sorry I let you girls down by forgetting my trunk," Jessie said. "But maybe I can help make up for it. While I was listing your ideas, I thought of a way to combine all of your suggestions into one super Big Idea."

"How?" some of the girls asked at the same time.

"Me and My Buddy could be the name for all of your ideas," Jessie said. "One camper who's good or strong at something helps another camper who isn't. Since everybody's good at something, and everybody needs a little help at other things, we all get to help our Buddies or have a Buddy help us."

After the Dolphins added more ideas, Jessie tapped her pencil against the wooden beam over her bed. "Hear! Hear!" Jessie began. She read off the list: " 'Teach Someone to Make Her Bed. Teach Somebody How to Do Something Hard. Help a Friend to Not Be Afraid of the Dark.' "

Jessie kept writing until her girls couldn't think of anything else. "Those will all be part of our Me and My Buddy Big Idea."

The chattering started up again as the girls talked about who could be Buddies for each other. They didn't notice that not everyone was still in the cabin. A few minutes later, they heard a knock on the door.

Ginny stepped into Cedar Cabin. "Inspection." She began to look around. She noticed how tidy everything was. All the trunks were shut. All the beds were made. All the sand and cobwebs had been swept away.

"Nice work, Dolphins," Ginny said. "Except for Jessie's wayward trunk, I'm giving you full points for a perfect cabin. Then Ginny noticed everything wasn't quite perfect in Cedar Cabin. "Goodness, Jessie, where's Lizzie?"

All eyes turned to Jessie. She got up from her bed and ran to the porch. "She was here just a second ago." Jessie looked down. Lizzie's sneakers were gone, with Lizzie in them!

"I'll need to talk with you about this,"

Ginny said. "I'm in a bit of a rush, but I'll wait here a few minutes while you go find her. Check the Bogs first."

Jessie headed to the girls' bathrooms. When she arrived, several of Kim's Seals were busy filling a water bucket with soapy water. Violet spotted Jessie in the mirror.

"Kim told us we have to wash down the cabin floor," Violet explained. "She said we didn't have any good activities for the Big Idea. I guess she wants us to get lots of points for making our cabin super clean. We have to hurry."

"Sorry," Jessie said. "Did you happen to see Lizzie in here?"

Violet nodded. "Not here, but she was in Birch when we all came to the Bogs. Want me to get her?"

"No, I'll go," Jessie answered.

Jessie stopped by Birch Cabin. Kim looked up. "If you're looking for Lizzie, she left for the ferry."

Jessie got to the point. "We need to talk with Lizzie about not coming here without

telling me. If we both talk to her, we can explain that the groups have to stay together for safety reasons."

"Fine," Kim said. "But I can't help it if she wants to be in my group and not yours. Anyway, she went to see her brother and her dad. It's not a big deal."

But it did turn out to be a big deal. When Jessie came back to Cedar Cabin alone, Ginny stepped onto the porch. "Jes-sie, it's time for the day campers to go back to Dark Harbor. Camp Seagull isn't just about the Olympics. It's also about responsibility. Lizzie is your responsibility."

Jessie looked down at her flip-flops. First her trunk was missing. Now one of her campers was missing. "I know. She already went to the ferry. I . . . uh . . . guess we'll meet her there."

Ginny's face grew very serious. "After the ferry leaves, ask Sarah to watch the cabin. Then please take some time to go over the rules about knowing where your campers are at all times. It's our most important safety rule."

To Jessie, every word that Ginny said felt like a stone falling on her head. "I know. I'm so sorry. I'll be much more careful."

Jessie walked slightly ahead of her Dolphins as they made their way to the ferry. She didn't want them to see that she was upset.

Henry's group caught up with Jessie's.

"What's the matter, Jessie?" Henry asked.

Jessie took a deep breath to steady her voice. "Lizzie left the cabin without telling me. I overheard her tell Zach she wants to be in Kim's cabin. Then I didn't know where she was when Ginny came by. When she and Kim don't follow the rules, I'm the one who looks like I don't know what I'm doing, and my campers lose points, too."

Henry nodded. "Same here, Jessie. Only Zach's the one who makes me feel like I shouldn't be here — like he's in charge of Camp Seagull or something. He won't do anything with the Dolphins."

CHAPTER 7

The Disappearing Flags

The next day, Henry Alden didn't need an alarm clock to wake up. When Dave Baylor, the Senior Counselor, arrived to supervise the campers in Driftwood Cabin, Henry was already up and dressed.

"Rich was right about you Aldens being early birds," Dave said. "I'll make sure you get points toward the Rise and Shine Medal."

Henry grinned. "We could use those points. I left my trunk at the ferry in Dark

Harbor," he told Dave. "I slept in my clothes, so that saved time. I always get up early, though."

Dave sat down on Henry's cot. "So does everybody around here. Just blast Rich's tape recorder with that bugle music. I guarantee campers will jump out of their beds like bedbugs. I'll get everybody in Driftwood Cabin around the flagpole by seven. That's when Boo brings over the day campers on the ferry. See you."

Camp Seagull was still quiet when Henry walked toward Evergreen Lodge. On the way, he went by Cedar Cabin, hoping to see Jessie. Like her brother, she was an early bird.

Sure enough, she was up and saw Henry go by. She stuck her head out the window over her bed.

"Hi, Jess," Henry whispered. "I see you slept in your clothes, too. I sure didn't like having my campers find out I left my trunk in Dark Harbor. Makes me look as if I don't know what I'm doing."

"I know," Jessie said miserably. "I can't

stop thinking about last night when Ginny told me to look over the rules about watching the campers. I already know the rules. The problem is, I can't get Lizzie and Kim to follow them. I'll see you later."

Henry went to the storage room when he got to Evergreen Lodge. He found the tape recorder and an extension cord. He plugged it in and brought the recorder outside. He pressed the start button. Then he blocked both ears.

The awful recorded bugle music drowned out the peaceful sounds of the ocean lapping in the distance. Two seagulls on the roof of Evergreen Lodge flew away in a hurry.

Henry checked his watch, then he returned to the storage room. "Where are those flags, anyway?" Henry said to himself as he looked around. "I know I put them in here last night after the campfire." He checked the shelves, then the closet. Nothing.

By this time, Ginny and Rich had arrived at their office.

"Morning, Henry," Rich said. "Mr. Pines will be here with your trunks when the ferry arrives. After the Flag Ceremony, you can bring them to the cabins."

Henry still felt bad about the missing trunks. He sure didn't want to tell the Gullens that the flags were missing, too.

"It'll be great to hear you blow a real bugle when your trunk gets here," Ginny told Henry. "That tape is pretty worn out by now. Our cat hides under the bed when she hears it."

"So do some of our campers!" Rich said with a laugh. "Live or recorded, the bugle wake-up is a Camp Seagull tradition."

Ginny smiled at Henry. "You did a nice job during the Flag Ceremony after the campfire last night, Henry. This morning the campers will watch the flag-raising, then sing the Camp Seagull song." Ginny paused. "What's the matter, Henry? Are you nervous? Don't be. You'll do fine again."

Henry shifted from one foot to the other. "Well, you see . . . actually, I can't find the flags right now. I remember folding them after the ceremony last night. I thought I put them away with the tape recorder. But now they're not in the storage room."

Henry noticed a tiny frown pass over Ginny's face. This was the same look she'd given the Aldens when she discovered their trunks had been left behind.

"Oh, dear," Ginny said quietly. "Rich and I will look around here. Run back to your cabin. See if you brought them there by mistake."

As campers streamed toward the flagpole, Henry dashed off to his cabin. Those flags just had to be there!

"Where're you going?" Henry's Driftwood Dolphins wanted to know when they saw him going the other way.

Jessie and Violet wanted to know the same thing when Henry passed by.

"Henry, it's almost seven o'clock," Jessie said. "Did you forget something in your cabin?"

Henry pulled Jessie to the side. "Did you notice what I did with the flags last night? I can't find them anywhere. I'm almost a hundred percent sure I put them in Evergreen Lodge with the tape recorder. But they're not there now."

Jessie was upset for her brother. "I feel terrible. There was so much going on that I didn't see where you went or what you did. Sorry."

Zach came over to Jessie and Henry. "Your trunks are by the dock. Aren't you supposed to be in charge of the Flag Ceremony right now?" He checked his watch. "It's in ten minutes. Flag Ceremony is always at seven o'clock in the morning — unless Ginny and Rich changed that, too."

Jessie's Dolphins looked confused by the delay. "Come along," she said, leading her campers toward the flagpole.

"Hurry up!" Kim ordered her group. "You can't be late for Flag Ceremony or we'll lose points."

Henry tried not to panic. Still, his heart was racing. "I have only a few minutes." He burst into Driftwood Cabin. He checked around as best he could in the short time he had. "It's no use. I know I didn't bring those flags here."

He felt sick inside. He didn't want to let down the whole camp. All he wanted was to set his eyes on those two flags. He wanted to listen to the hush that would come over the campers as he raised the flags to begin the day.

He turned back toward Evergreen Lodge. His legs felt like wooden blocks. As he ran back, he had a new dark thought: *The Dolphins are probably going to have a trillion points taken away from them because I lost those flags.*

When he came to the clearing, Henry saw the expectant campers waiting for him. The ferry had brought in the day campers. He saw Benny waving.

Henry's mind slowed down. What was he going to say to everyone? How could he tell them that, for the first time ever, Camp Seagull wouldn't be starting the day with the Flag Ceremony?

As he was trying to come up with the words, Jessie appeared. Trailing behind were some of the Cedar Cabin Dolphins. Jessie was grinning from ear to ear.

"Did you find the flags?" Henry asked, barely able to get the words out.

Daisy handed Henry two stiff posters. "Here. Jessie told us what to do. She found some poster board in the arts and crafts room, and markers, too. We drew the flags on them. The flags aren't very pretty. We only had time to draw a bunch of lines."

Henry couldn't believe his eyes when he saw the two hand-drawn flags. One of them had a bird in the middle that almost looked like the one on the Camp Seagull flag. The other had stars and stripes — most of them, anyway.

"Thanks," Henry said to the Cedar Cabin Dolphins. "These are the nicest flags I've ever seen."

Rich made a move to start up the bugle tape. "They're almost as nice as the real ones, Henry," he said, "wherever they are. Ginny just gave the Dolphins twenty-five points for the Quick Thinking Award. Of course, losing the flags cost you twenty

points, but you Dolphins made a five-point gain anyway." With that, Rich blasted the recorded bugle music to get everyone's attention. It was time for the famous Camp Seagull Flag Ceremony.

Henry attached the handmade flags to the ropes and pulled them gently. Up went the Stars and Stripes. Up went the Camp Seagull flag, which was soon flapping in the wind.

"*Crawk! Crawk!*" some of the campers cried when the flag reached the top.

Everyone cheered the Cedar Cabin Dolphins, who had saved the day. Then they gave a cheer for Henry Alden, to make him feel better.

Well, not quite everyone. When Jessie looked around to check on Lizzie, she noticed she was over with Zach and Kim near the dock. They were sitting on the Aldens' trunks, and they weren't cheering at all.

CHAPTER 8

The Switch

After the Flag Ceremony, Henry and Jessie fetched their trunks. They quickly dropped them off at their cabins. In no time, they caught up to everyone heading to Evergreen Lodge for breakfast. It was Blueberry Pancake Day. Nobody wanted to miss that!

Jessie's and Henry's tables were next to each other. Luckily for Violet, Kim's table was nearby as well. The Aldens liked meeting new campers. But they also liked seeing one another at camp.

Jessie turned around to see how Benny was doing. "Are you going to eat that whole stack of blueberry pancakes?" she asked.

Benny wiped some sticky maple syrup from the corners of his mouth. "Grandfather said I should only have a tiny piece of toast in case my stomach did flip-flops on the ferry. I saved being hungry for breakfast at camp."

"I guess you did, by the look of your plate," Henry said. "Now the Dolphins don't have to worry about losing points for the No Food on the Floor Award."

A loud drumming sound boomed over the noisy dining hall. Ginny was onstage banging a metal serving spoon against a metal soup pot from the camp kitchen.

"I think Ginny and Rich are about to announce who won the Big Idea," Jessie said. "I hope the Dolphins have a good chance."

Daisy squeezed Jessie's hand. "I can't wait. Maybe our cabin will win. Do you want to know what our idea is?" Daisy asked a boy Dolphin at Henry's table.

"Shhhh, no telling," Jessie told Daisy just in time.

After everyone finally quieted down, Ginny tapped the microphone. "I know you're all eager to find out who the Big Idea winner is. We won't keep you waiting any longer. As your counselors told you, for our new Olympics we asked all the cabins to think up ways to make Camp Seagull the best ever. The Big Idea Medal is for the best of the bunch — the idea that pulls the whole camp together."

Ginny stepped away from the microphone so Rich could speak. "We were up half the night trying to decide on the winner. There were so many great entries, we'd have to run Camp Seagull all year 'round to try them all out. Now, after I announce the idea we chose, I'd like the winning counselor to come up. Drumroll, please."

Ginny banged on the soup pot again. The campers banged on their tables with their silverware. Evergreen Lodge was jumping!

"And the winner is . . . Me and My Buddy!" Rich yelled into the microphone.

"We won! We won!" the Dolphins at Jessie's table yelled.

"We won! We won!" the Seals at Kim's table yelled.

Ginny banged the soup pot again to get everyone's attention. "For the first time this summer, we have two identical outstanding ideas," Ginny announced when everyone quieted down. "Because Me and My Buddy is so special, I'd like to recognize Jessie's Dolphins. Come up here and take a bow, Jessie."

Jessie stepped onstage, confused. The audience was confused, too. Only a few campers clapped.

"Now let's hear it for the Seals, who submitted their idea first," Ginny cried. "Come on up for your group, Kim."

"What? No fair," one Dolphin after another muttered.

Jessie tried to say something to make her campers feel better, but her lips wouldn't move.

Ginny tapped the microphone with her pencil. "Now, now. Let's all be good sports. It's only fair to give the medal to the group that came up with the idea first."

Rich took the microphone. "I hereby award one hundred points to the Seals, along with a special banner to the girls of Birch Cabin." Rich shook Kim's hand, then gave her the Cabin of the Week banner. "The Seals move to the front in the Olympics. Let's hear it for the Seals and for Birch!"

The Birch Cabin Seals ran to the stage. They helped Kim hold up the banner.

"Go, Seals!" the Seals roared.

When the cheering died down, Rich explained the winning idea and then made the morning announcements. "Now it's time to clean your tables and bring your plates to the kitchen. Then you'll return to your cabins for morning cabin inspection. After that, everyone goes to activities. Meanwhile, we hope you will find Buddies and Buddies will find you to help each other the rest of the week."

The Dolphins were quiet as they cleared their tables.

Jessie wiped up every drip and speck. She didn't want the Dolphins to fall further behind. "I'm so sorry I somehow let you down," Jessie said to the girls as they were cleaning up. "I never thought someone else would come up with our same idea and that I should have gotten it to Ginny before the Seals did."

Jessie's Dolphins were too disappointed to say anything.

"Dolphins," Henry said to make everyone feel better, "the Seals are ahead now, but this is only the beginning of camp."

"I'll be your Buddy, Jessie," Daisy said as the group walked back to the cabins for inspection.

This made Jessie smile. "If there's a Big Heart Award, you'll win it, Daisy." She turned to the other Dolphins. "Here are your schedules for today's activities. Start walking to the first activity. Henry and I will meet you there in a few minutes."

"Can I stay with you?" Benny asked his brother and sister. "Henry gave me my schedule already. Look, here comes Violet."

The four Aldens stood on the porch without speaking. They looked at the campers below, who were excited to start the day. Were they ever going to feel that way about Camp Seagull?

"We just arrived at camp," Jessie began, "and too many things keep happening that don't make sense. First our trunks are left behind. Next you can't find the flags, Henry. Then Kim's group somehow comes up with the same idea as the Dolphins."

"And Lizzie doesn't obey and keeps on disappearing," Henry said. "Don't forget that."

"Right," Jessie went on. "I have a feeling she and Kim tried to scare the Dolphins with the monster footprints so we'd lose points for screaming. But the big thing is what just happened. I have a feeling Kim somehow got Me and My Buddy from our group. But how?"

Henry looked at Violet. "I know you can't really talk about how your cabin decided on its Big Idea. But did anything happen that seemed suspicious?"

Jessie stopped her sister before she could

answer. "Violet, you really shouldn't say anything about this."

Violet wanted to help, but she stopped herself. She knew Jessie was right.

Henry shook his head and said, "There's got to be a way to find out if Kim copied you."

Jessie turned to Violet. "It's time to send you on your way," she said. "It wouldn't be fair for you to hear our plans for solving this mystery."

Violet walked slowly back to her cabin.

Benny looked over at Henry. Henry's eyebrows were scrunched together. Benny knew what that meant. Henry was cooking up a plan.

Henry began, "On Costume Night, we'll let the Dolphins think we're going to dress up one way, but we'll really have secret costumes!"

"You mean, we'll tell everybody we're going to be ghosts, but then we'll be pirates?" Benny asked.

"Exactly!" Henry said. "The only problem is figuring out how to let Ginny and Rich know what our real costumes are ahead of time."

"We could give them a letter in an envelope beforehand," Jessie suggested, "and tell them not to open it until after the costume contest. If somebody shows up with the same costumes, then they'll know who the copycats are."

"Not the Aldens," Benny said. "We're not copycats."

"Let's do it," Henry said.

CHAPTER 9

Secret Disguises

For the next two days, Henry, Jessie, and Benny were busy every minute. They worked hard to win points and to pull close to the Seals in the Olympics.

The Dolphins won the most points for all the cabin inspections. They picked up the First One in the Freezing Water at Swimming Lessons Medal. When they decorated their fruits like circus clowns, they won the Dress Up Your Favorite Fruit Medal. Benny picked up ten points all by himself. He made people laugh more than any other camper. His table didn't lose a single point for dropping food on the floor, either. As the week went on, the Dolphins were catching up to the Seals.

Jessie checked the points board one morning after the Flag Ceremony. "I sure wish you could find those flags, Henry. Maybe Rich and Ginny would give the Dolphins back some of the points you lost after they disappeared."

Henry groaned. "Uh, don't mention those. My cabin is trying to sew another seagull flag, but they haven't gotten very far. They're too busy working on their costumes. Plus I'm busy working on two sets of costumes for the Dolphin boys — the secret ones and the fake ones."

"Well, I'd help you, but I'm busy with our girls' costumes," Jessie whispered. "I stayed up half the night with my flashlight by my side making a lobster head out of a cardboard box. I found some old oven mitts the kitchen was throwing out. So I made claws out of them. I can only work on the costumes while my campers are asleep. I'm so tired I can hardly keep my eyes open."

"Well, I've got a little free time now," Henry told Jessie. "Dave's at the playing field with our campers. That means I'll have the cabin to myself to finish the secret costumes. I'm making underwater creature headpieces out of boxes I've been sneaking from the office trash."

"My costume's easy," Benny whispered so no one walking by would overhear. "The other kids think I'm making an astronaut suit from the gray sweatshirt Dave gave me. But it's going to be a whale outfit."

"Sounds good," Henry told Benny. "My campers are going wild on their space outfits. Wait until I tell them they have to be lobsters and sharks and clams, not space aliens. I hid the masks and headpieces way under the cabin. Rich and Ginny never check there during cabin inspection. We still haven't had a surprise inspection yet, so we have to be on the lookout all the time."

"What about the letter to Ginny and Rich?" Jessie asked.

"Done!" Henry pulled a sheet of lined

paper from his pocket. He looked around. "Good. Nobody's coming. I'll read it to you."

Dear Ginny and Rich,

The Dolphins would like to register our idea for Costume Night ahead of time. Everybody thinks we're going to be space creatures. But we will really show up as underwater creatures.

Yours truly,
Henry Alden

"That sounds fine," Jessie said. "Here's the envelope I wrote. It says: 'To Be Opened After Costume Night Begins.' We'll give it to Ginny and Rich tomorrow."

"I wish we could tell Violet about our plan," Benny said when he saw her walking toward him. "I like it when we all have the same secret."

Violet seemed shy around her sister and brothers now that they had secrets from her. "Hi," she said. "Is it okay to visit with you?"

Henry gave his sister a hug. "Sure thing,

Violet. Being on different teams isn't much fun."

Benny had a question. "What are your costumes?"

Violet grinned, then shook her head. "Teams aren't allowed to tell each other their ideas."

"Can you tell if Kim picked one of your ideas?" Benny asked. "You always made the best costumes for the Greenfield Halloween parade."

Violet nodded. "I did give Kim one idea. We started on it. But since your team has gotten so many points in the last couple of days, she was afraid my idea wasn't strong enough to win. All of a sudden, she came up with something else. That's what our cabin is working on now. I can't say what it is."

Henry was proud of his sister for keeping her cabin's secret. "Okay, Violet. Hey, there's Zach. We'd better all leave.

"Oh, hi," Henry said when Zach came out of the camp office with an armload of papers. "Anything for me?"

As usual, Zach answered Henry with as few words as possible. "No."

Henry turned to Benny. "Let's go to the playing field. I told Dave I'd drop you off. Afterward I'll be at the cabin."

"Can't I help finish some of those shark heads?" Benny asked.

"Shhh." Henry pointed to Zach. He was still nearby, reading notices on the camp bulletin board.

"Oops," Benny whispered before he and Henry left.

After dropping off Benny at the field, Henry returned to Driftwood Cabin. He looked around, and then he crawled under the cabin. He had hidden several trash bags filled with cardboard, paint, and materials from the arts and crafts room. He was still under the cabin with his legs sticking out when he heard Rich's voice nearby.

"Surprise inspection!" Rich announced, laughing. "I know you Dolphins want to win the Olympics, but you don't have to clean under the cabin, whoever you are."

"Ouch!" Henry cried as he bumped his

head crawling out backward. "It's me."

Rich gave Henry a once-over. "Henry, good thing this is cabin inspection, not Junior Counselor inspection. You're covered with dirt and pine needles."

Henry looked down at himself. His knees and elbows were sandy. He had cobwebs in his hair. There were pine needles stuck to his clothes. "Sorry, Rich."

"I didn't expect to find anyone here," Rich said. "Everybody's at activities. What were you doing under the cabin, anyway? Did you drop something down there?"

"Oh, I . . . uh . . . had a free period," Henry began, "and came here to work on our costumes. I, uh . . . lost a sewing needle through the floorboards."

Rich thought this was funny. "Did you really expect to find something that small down there, Henry? Ginny and I should check under all the cabins. That's probably where all our lost things go."

This made Henry nervous. "Uh, no. There's nothing but pine needles under there." He brushed himself off and went up the porch stairs. He hoped Rich didn't get any more ideas about checking under the cabin. "I'll stand out on the porch while you do the surprise inspection. I don't want to mess up the cabin after we just cleaned it."

Rich went inside. "Looking good, Henry. Beds tight. Trunks under the bed. Towels hung up on the railing. Flags on the . . . bed! The flags! What are they doing on your bed?"

Henry forgot about messing up the cabin. He raced inside. What was Rich talking about? "My campers were trying to make a new Camp Seagull flag, but they didn't get very far."

Rich unfolded the large cloth flag he'd found on Henry's bed. "I'd say your campers did a pretty good likeness of the camp seagull. Take a look."

Henry couldn't believe his eyes. "That's the real flag that was missing!"

"Here's the other one," Rich said, unrolling the Stars and Stripes. "How come you were keeping them in your cabin? These belong in Evergreen Lodge."

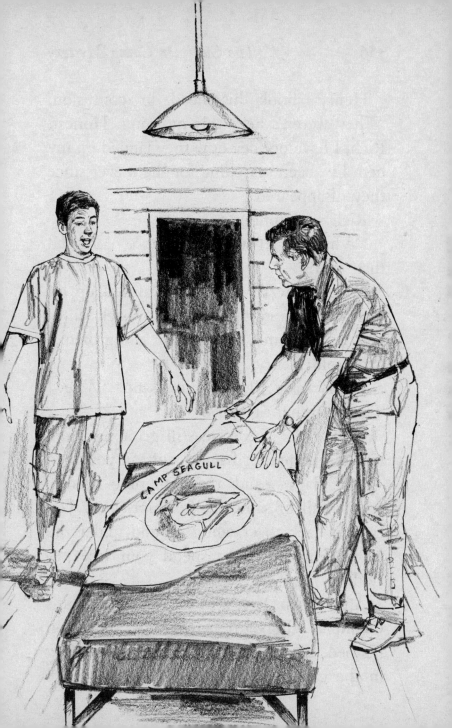

Henry shook his head in confusion. "They weren't here this morning. Honest, Rich. I have no idea how they landed on my bed. I've been searching for them ever since they disappeared."

Rich was smiling.

"What?" Henry asked, more confused than ever.

"Well, now that the flags turned up on your bed, I'm going to give you back ten of the twenty points you lost for losing them," Rich told Henry.

Henry gave Rich a thumbs-up. "Whew! That's a relief. Thanks."

"But," Rich went on, still grinning, "you lose ten points for having stuff on your bed — the flags — and a pile of pine needles and a trail of sand on the floor. Now you can go back to crawling around under the cabin. Funny way to spend your free period."

After Rich left with the flags and his Olympics clipboard, Henry sat down on his bed. That's when he noticed something in the cabin mailbox on the wall. A piece of paper was sticking out that hadn't been there in the morning.

Henry took the paper. "A schedule change," he said. Then an idea hit him. "I bet Zach delivered this when I went to the playing field with Benny," Henry said to himself. "I wonder if he had anything to do with those flags showing up."

CHAPTER 10

Costume Night

The girls in Birch Cabin gathered around Violet. "Can you be my costume Buddy?" a girl named Maggie asked. "You helped me with the candy dish I made in pottery. I need a Buddy again for my costume. Kim's too busy."

Kim raced around the cabin looking for pins and glue and scissors for her own costume. "Hurry up with the girls, Violet," she said. "We have to be at Evergreen Lodge soon. I want to be at the front of the costume parade. The Styrofoam on my headpiece doesn't look right. I'm supposed to be a scary alien, but I look like a television set."

Kim wasn't the friendliest counselor at Camp Seagull. The girls weren't sure whether or not to laugh. Finally, they couldn't help it. Kim *did* look like a Styrofoam television set, not a space alien.

Kim finally looked pleased with her campers. "Well, now I know I'm going to win for best costume idea. Usually campers just dress up like ghosts or witches, but being space aliens is much better. Uh-oh! Where's the spaceship? You need to put on your spaceship, Violet. Oh, I'm ready to scream, but I can't, or we'll lose points."

Violet calmly walked to the broom closet. "Here it is."

"It's beautiful, Violet," Maggie said.

Indeed, the spaceship Violet had made was a silvery beauty. She had covered two long sheets of poster board with silver paint. There was an opening for her face and a spaceship window drawn around it. All Violet had to do was sandwich herself between the two sides.

"It's nice," Kim said. This was the first time she'd said anything kind to Violet.

In Driftwood Cabin, Henry had his hands full with some very confused Dolphins.

"Why am I a lobster?" one boy asked as Henry put on red gloves that were supposed to be claws. "I thought I was going to be a space alien."

Benny's eyes grew larger than usual. "Somebody might copy our idea. That's why we made something different — to fool them."

"Who?" the lobster camper asked.

"We don't know for sure," Henry said. "So we decided to change into secret costumes. Now promise you won't bite anyone."

The sea creatures laughed. They had fun waving their cardboard fins and claws at one another.

Cedar Cabin was filling up with underwater creatures, including a goldfish, a horseshoe crab, and even a scary stingray.

"We just have to wait for Lizzie to get here," Jessie said. "She's helping her dad with the ferry. He's making a few trips to bring out all the parents and grandparents for Costume Night."

"Lizzie's going to be surprised when she finds out she's a sea turtle, not an astronaut," Daisy said.

Jessie smiled as she put on her own dolphin headpiece. "Shhh, I think she's coming up the steps."

"What's going on?" Lizzie asked when she stepped inside. "Am I in the wrong cabin or something?"

Jessie found the poster-board turtle shell she had made in secret. "It's a sea turtle costume. See, you just tie it around your waist."

"We're supposed to be aliens, not sea turtles!" Lizzie cried. "I promised."

"Promised whom?" Jessie asked in a serious voice.

Before Lizzie could answer, the girls heard more footsteps.

"Shut the door," Jessie said. "It might be one of the Seals coming to take a look. "Who is it?" she asked when there was a knock at the door.

"Benny the Whale and Henry the Shark," a boy's voice answered. "Open up, or we'll swallow your cabin!"

The girls burst into giggles.

Jessie opened the door.

"Time to go," Henry said, speaking through his shark head. "The rest of my cabin is outside."

"Hey, where's your costume, Lizzie?" Benny asked. "Aren't you going to be a sea turtle like Jessie told me?"

The sea turtle costume lay on Lizzie's bed, untouched. Instead, she grabbed her astronaut helmet. "I'm not going to Costume Night as a sea turtle. This is my costume."

The campers entered Evergreen Lodge cabin group by cabin group. Kim led her Seals at the front of the costume parade. She had a big confident smile when the audience cheered the space aliens. The Birch Cabin campers stepped to the side to watch the rest of the parade.

Pirates and goblins and even a couple of campers dressed as Monster Rock paraded in. Campers cheered for one another.

When Henry's and Jessie's Dolphins came in, the cheers were the loudest of all.

Then Benny tapped Jessie's dolphin fin to get her attention. "Look at Kim. Her face is all red. She's not clapping anymore. She's too mad to clap."

"What's going on, Lizzie?" Kim asked when the Dolphins passed the Seals. "You told me the kids in your cabin were coming as space aliens!"

The Dolphins turned around. Lizzie had joined the parade, after all — not as an astronaut but as a sea turtle! She actually liked the sea turtle costume better.

Ginny and Rich had been standing near Kim's group and had overheard her question to Lizzie.

"What do you mean, Kim?" Ginny asked. "Did Lizzie tell you what the Dolphins were planning to wear? Please explain yourself."

Kim's space alien headpiece fell sideways on her head. She sputtered and tried to straighten it out.

"Does anyone know what's going on?" Ginny asked. "I'm going to have Rich make an announcement to the audience that we are serving refreshments first. In the meantime, I want to get to the bottom of this."

Jessie stepped away from her campers. "Did you find the letter we put in your mailbox, Ginny? It might explain this mixup better than what anyone tells you."

Rich overheard this. He handed Ginny the Aldens' letter. Ginny read it over and looked at Henry and Jessie, puzzled. "You mean you *knew* Birch Cabin was going to copy your costumes? Why would you think that?"

"Because they copied Jessie's Big Idea," Benny blurted out.

Kim seemed to shrink back when Benny said this.

"Was Me and My Buddy really Jessie's idea, Kim?" Ginny asked.

Kim nodded. "Yes. I couldn't think of anything good for that or for the costumes, either. I'm just good at sports, not the new things you and Rich want us to do. Everything is different from the way Camp Seagull used to be. Lizzie told me about Me and My Buddy, so I raced to your office to make sure I submitted it before Jessie got hers in."

"What about you, Lizzie?" Ginny asked. "Did you have anything to do with that — and with telling Kim about the Dolphins' costumes?"

Lizzie looked like a very unhappy sea turtle. "I did tell Kim about Me and My Buddy so her group would win, not the Aldens'. And I told her about the Dolphins being space aliens, too. But the Aldens fooled everybody."

Jessie looked at Lizzie. "We can't figure out why you don't seem to want us to have a good time at Camp Seagull."

Lizzie stood there, not saying anything. That's when Zach Pines stepped forward from the crowd of campers. "It's not hard to figure out. Lizzie and I were supposed to be overnight campers. Then, at the last minute, Ginny and Rich gave our overnight places to you. My dad's family owned Camp Seagull for a long time, and now Ginny and Rich have taken it over." Zach put his arm around his sister, which wasn't too easy to do because of her turtle shell.

"I was worried I'd never get to be an overnight camper," Lizzie said. "There are four of you and only two of us. So I did things that would make everybody think you shouldn't be counselors. Then maybe you wouldn't be asked back."

"Did you take the flags, too, Lizzie?" Henry asked.

Lizzie looked confused. "The flags? No."

"I did," Zach confessed. "Just for a little while. Then my dad found them in my room at home. He put them back in your cabin yesterday. Flag Ceremony was my favorite job, but then the Gullens gave it to you. My dad and other people in my family always did Flag Ceremony. That's my uncle playing on the bugle tape. I know it doesn't sound as good as Henry's bugle, but it sounds good to us."

Rich walked over to Zach. "I tried to take some responsibility away from you so you could enjoy camp more and not work so hard. I didn't realize I had hurt you. Next year, you can be in charge of Flag Ceremony again."

"We didn't know you were upset about not being overnight campers. We promise we'll make room for you next summer," added Ginny.

"And Zach, I'll teach you how to play the bugle," Henry said. "That reminds me — what about our trunks? Did you leave our trunks behind on purpose the first day? Or was it you, Kim?"

Kim and Zach shook their heads.

"I was so busy, I just forgot them on the beach," Kim said. "I guess I was glad that you would lose points for the Dolphins because you didn't remember to take your trunks. But it wasn't on purpose."

"Same here," Zach confessed. "I saw them on the beach before my dad started the ferry. But I didn't do anything to get them, either. Sorry."

"How about the monster footprints?" Jessie asked.

Lizzie and Kim exchanged looks.

"I did that!" Lizzie said. "It's allowed. Ever since there was a Camp Seagull, we could do pranks to make people scream. You and Rich didn't change that, did you, Ginny?"

"Not really," Ginny answered. "Even when I worked at the camp when I was your age, we had pranks about the monster of Camp Seagull. But not on the first couple of nights. We weren't supposed to scare the new campers until after they were settled in."

"We weren't scared!" the Dolphin girls of Cedar Cabin cried.

"But I am. Some of you are very scary!"

Ginny said, looking around at the sharks, stingrays, and space aliens. "I really don't know which group should take the costume prize."

The score between the Seals and the Dolphins was very close. The Dolphins only needed fifty points to win and the costume contest was worth a hundred points. If Ginny automatically let the Dolphins win because of Kim's poor sportsmanship, that would be unfair to the Seal campers. Ginny turned to Kim, Lizzie, and Zach, and continued, "I don't want the Seals or the Dolphins to be penalized by your actions. But I do think that the three of you owe the camp an apology for your behavior during this Olympics."

The three nodded in agreement.

Benny broke the tension when he piped up, "I've got a good idea. It's not a Big Idea, but a little one 'cause I'm only six."

"What is it?" Rich asked.

"Let the people who are watching us in the audience vote," Benny suggested. "They can write down which team they think has the best costumes. Then we can count up the votes."

Rich and Ginny looked at each other.

"You were wrong, Benny," Rich said. "That is a Big Idea."

After Rich made the announcement about the voting, Ginny handed out slips of paper to the audience. Then Rich sent around some of the campers to collect the votes.

After refreshments, Ginny came out with her soup pot and her serving spoon and banged them together.

"The votes are in! Rich and I will now give the award to the team for the best costumes," she announced.

"Drumroll, please," Rich said.

Ginny banged on the soup pot.

"The Best Costume Award goes to . . . the Dolphins!"

Since Jessie was dressed as a dolphin, she led her group up to the stage. "Thank you," she said to Rich and Ginny when they put a medal around her dolphin neck.

"The Dolphins are also our Olympic

winners!" Ginny announced. "Here's the gold medal."

Jessie pushed Benny forward. "You thought up the costume voting, Benny. You go over and get the medal."

Ginny was careful when she lowered the medal over Benny's head. She didn't want to disturb the cardboard tube he was wearing as part of his whale outfit.

"Let's hear it for the Dolphins!" Rich said.

"Let's hear it for whales, too!" Benny said.

GERTRUDE CHANDLER WARNER discovered when she was teaching that many readers who like an exciting story could find no books that were both easy and fun to read. She decided to try to meet this need, and her first book, *The Boxcar Children*, quickly proved she had succeeded.

Miss Warner drew on her own experiences to write the mystery. As a child she spent hours watching trains go by on the tracks opposite her family home. She often dreamed about what it would be like to set up housekeeping in a caboose or freight car—the situation the Alden children find themselves in.

While the mystery element is central to each of Miss Warner's books, she never thought of them as strictly juvenile mysteries. She liked to stress the Aldens' independence and resourcefulness and their solid New England devotion to using up and making do. The Aldens go about most of their adventures with as little adult supervision as possible—something else that delights young readers.

Miss Warner lived in Putnam, Connecticut, until her death in 1979. During her lifetime, she received hundreds of letters from girls and boys telling her how much they liked her books.